Doc Dudley's Daughter

Elisabeth Hamilton Friermood

Doubleday & Company, Inc.
Garden City, New York

Gratefully dedicated
to
Margaret Lesser
who, for fifteen years, edited my books
with patience and understanding.

E.H.F.

Contents

8 Contents

Acknowledgments

Harper City's acquisition of a Carnegie library building at the turn of the century is similar to the event that took place at the same time in my home town, Marion, Indiana, where long ago I served as a children's librarian.

Records of how Marion obtained its library building and newspaper accounts of its dedication ceremony were supplied by a member of the Marion Public Library staff, a long-time friend, Meriel Bower.

Along with these early records, I was fortunate in having at hand magazines for 1898, lent by another friend, Jean Roehm, from her outstanding collection of historical periodicals.

The writing of this tale has been satisfyingly nostalgic. How easy and pleasant to recall every room, every corridor, every white marble step and column of Mr. Carnegie's grand gift to my town!

E.H.F.

Chapter 1

A Diploma at Last

Em squirmed on the uncomfortable folding chair. Why didn't Mr. Wrightson get on with it? It had been such a long evening!

Crowded with the parents and friends of the graduating class, the Masonic Hall was warm. There had been too many orations and recitations by the seniors, and the superintendent of schools' speech, "The Future Is Yours," had been tiresome and preachy.

At last, taking one of the rolled, ribbon-tied diplomas from the table beside him, Mr. Wrightson, the high school principal, called her name, "Emeline Louisa Dudley."

Em wadded her handkerchief into a tight ball, got to her feet, and walked across the platform. The three starched, flounced petticoats under her white graduation dress made an audible swish as they swayed below her ankles.

The principal smiled as he handed her the diploma and said, "Congratulations, Emeline."

"Thank you," she murmured and returned to the tormenting chair.

She looked at the long white diploma in her lap. It was over. She had graduated at last! With a head full of Latin, English Literature, Algebra, and History, she was supposed to be educated. At this moment she didn't feel so; she just felt hot and sticky and wished she hadn't laced her corset so tightly. Heavenly days! who would think it would take this long for twenty-seven seniors to get diplomas?

Em recrossed her ankles and glanced at Papa, Mama, and Vic in the back of the hall. Even as she looked a man came and tapped Papa on the shoulder. Papa nodded, spoke to Mama beside him, then rose and left.

Em sighed and turned her head to watch Mr. Wrightson hand Virginia Miller her diploma. Thank goodness, Em thought, her own name was at the beginning of the alphabet so that Papa had seen her get *her* diploma. Papa seldom got to stay to the end of anything, be it a church service or a play at the Opera House. She was proud to be Doc Dudley's daughter, but sometimes—

She glanced back at Mama and Vic. If only Ashton were sitting with them this graduation would be more exciting. Ashton had a way of giving her self-confidence, and of adding sparkle to the whole Dudley household. Few older brothers, she felt, could ever come up to Ashton. Thoughts of the war that had taken him from medical school riled her almost as much as they did Papa.

Now Mr. Wrightson took the last diploma from the table and turned to the audience.

"Judge Hargrove, will you please step forward and receive this diploma for Charles?"

The judge got up from his seat in the rear, walked down the aisle, and stood below the platform. The principal handed down the diploma.

"Judge," he said, "it is with great pleasure that I present you with your son's diploma. The class of '98 is honored to have one of its members serving our country with Roosevelt's Rough Riders. Would you care to give us any word about Charles?"

Her pulse beating a little faster, Em leaned forward.

Good-looking Charlie Hargrove had sat two desks in front of her in history class at the beginning of the semester. If it hadn't been for the war, he would be right here on this platform tonight and might be asking to walk home with her afterward. That pesky war!

Even before the sinking of the battleship *Maine* in the harbor at Havana, Cuba, last February, Charlie had talked in class about the wrong heaped upon Cuba by Spain. He had argued with their teacher, Mr. Wilson, that United States should rescue the nearby island from its persecutor. As Em remembered it, when Charlie talked heatedly, he was more handsome than ever.

Now she watched the judge. Gesticulating with Charlie's diploma, he turned to the audience and cleared his throat.

"Well, most of you have probably read the parts of Charlie's letters that have been printed in the *News*. In today's mail I received a letter from him telling that the regiment would soon be leaving San Antonio, Texas, for Tampa, Florida, where they will embark for Cuba. I expect the next letter he writes will be from Tampa."

Em sat back in her chair. It was a sore point with Papa and her that the editor of the *News* printed Charlie's letters and not Ashton's.

She looked down at Mr. Wilson, the history teacher, seated with a group of the faculty in the front row. She remembered Mr. Wilson's look of dismay last April, when she had announced in class that her older brother, Ashton, had answered President McKinley's call for volunteers by leaving medical school to join the army. She suspected that Mr. Wilson and Papa were the only men in town who were not enthusiastic about the war.

Em ran her finger under the stays that held her collar high and snug about her throat, then touched the fluffy, chiffon pom-pom at the back. Watching Judge Hargrove return to his seat amid applause, she thought how glad she would be to get out into the fresh air.

It was a relief to stand while Reverend Haley pronounced the benediction. When he finished, there was a rattling of chairs on the platform as the seniors spoke to one another.

"Emmy, what a beautiful watch! A graduation present?" Virginia Miller touched the gold watch pinned below the shoulder on Em's dress.

"Yes. Mama and Papa gave it to me just before we left home. See the engraving on the back?"

Virginia read aloud. "Emeline Dudley, May 27, 1898. That's nice, Em. But I guess you'd never forget this date even if you didn't have the watch to remind you. I know I'll never forget it. Wasn't it exciting having Charlie get his diploma that way? Terry Dawes is walking me home. I must find Mama and tell her. Anybody asked you yet?"

"No. Not yet." Em looked around. The three girls around Jeff Wayne were laughing at his jokes and enjoying his teasing, so—it didn't appear that *he* would be asking her. Virginia walked off with Terry and Em started toward the platform steps.

"Wait, Em."

Em looked up at Alex Thompson.

"May I walk you home?" he asked.

"Why, yes, thank you, Alex." This was a surprise. He had never asked to take her home before. Alex was tall, broad-shouldered, stolid and, as Mama once said, dependable; but not very exciting, according to Em's way of thinking. Still, she didn't know him really; he had come to very few of the senior class parties. Maybe she'd get to know him better tonight. "Mama's down there. I'll tell her you are taking me home."

By this time the hall resounded with the low rumble of conversation as the seniors joined their families, the girls in white dresses, the boys in dark suits and white shirts, the starched collars so high it was painful for them to turn their heads. Parents and grandparents, aunts and uncles passed around the unrolled diplomas to admire the fancy lettering and the signatures of the principal and superintendent.

Em elbowed her way up the aisle, Alex behind her. Mama and Vic stood at the end of their row of seats, waiting. Mama's summer hat was nice, Em thought. Its broad, flower-trimmed brim set off her round face very becomingly.

"Mama, Alex Thompson is going to take me home," Em said.

Mama looked beyond Em to Alex. Em watched a pleased expression spread over her mother's face. Em chuckled inwardly. Mama was so transparent, thinking, no doubt, how good it was that a "dependable" boy like Alex was taking her daughter home.

"Well, now, that's nice, Alex. How is your grandma? She wasn't here this evening, was she?" Mama asked.

"No, just my dad. Grandma's rheumatism keeps her home most of the time." Alex looked beyond Mrs. Dudley to Vic. "Say, young man, you look pretty sleepy."

Mama brushed back her son's hair. "He is, Alex. This is late for an eleven-year-old to be up. Way past his bedtime. Come on, Vic, I must get you home." Mama turned to Em. "Em, don't forget, I baked a fresh cake this afternoon. I'm sure Alex would like some. Well, good night."

"Oh, Mama, take my diploma, will you? It's proof that you have an educated daughter."

"I will, indeed, and tomorrow I shall take it downtown to be framed."

Em watched as Mama led sleepy Vic through the door. The crowd thinned out.

Alex stepped to Em's side. "Shall we go? It's awfully hot in here." He tugged at his collar.

Outside the air was soft and balmy, almost like June. The two descended the front steps and started down the street. Em cast a side glance at Alex but could only see his profile in the glow from the street lamp.

"Well, Alex," she said after a while, "what are you going to do now that you have graduated?" She had to make some kind of a start on conversation since Alex didn't seem so inclined.

"Just what I've always done, I expect, work for my dad."

"I'm sure your father will like that. Papa was so looking forward to the time when Ashton would finish medical school and come home to practice medicine with him." Em sighed. "But Ashton got so fired with patriotism and sympathy for Cuba that he enlisted at the first call for volunteers. Now heaven knows when he will finish his medical training."

"I tried to enlist too," Alex said, "tried to enlist at the same time Charlie Hargrove did. The only difference was that the judge signed Charlie's papers and my dad wouldn't. I'm not eighteen yet. The judge, you know, is a Harvard man, like Colonel Roosevelt, so he wrote to the colonel and Charlie got in the Rough Riders' regiment. I'll be eighteen in September, and, if the war isn't over by then, I'm going to enlist."

"Let's hope it's over soon and Ashton can get back to college," Em said.

They turned down Main Street and passed the Court House in the middle of the town square. Em remembered that just four weeks ago there had been wild jubilation in this square. Practically the whole town had turned out to celebrate Commodore Dewey's victory at the battle of

Manila Bay, in which he had captured the entire Spanish fleet in the Pacific and had taken the Philippines.

It was said that there hadn't been such excitement since the Civil War. And what a good war this was, Em had heard a patient say in Papa's office, because now the blue and gray were reunited in a common cause. Papa had replied wryly that there was no such thing as a good war. That had been the day he had received Ashton's letter telling of his enlistment. Em thought Papa had aged ten years in appearance since receiving that letter.

She knew how he felt about Ashton. Indeed, the whole family felt the same. Ashton was special. Seven years older than herself, he had never made her feel that she was a bother to him when they were growing up. Most older brothers, she knew, thought younger sisters nothing but pests. Once, playing catch with Vic, Ashton had said, "Vic, I shouldn't wonder but what you will be a great pitcher like Cy Young when you grow up." No wonder Vic worshiped him. Ashton, Papa said, was going to be a fine doctor.

"Where is Ashton?" Alex asked.

"At Camp Alger in Falls Church, Virginia," Em replied.

"How come the *News* hasn't published any of *his* letters?"

"Papa did take one down to the editor, Jake Rhorer, but he said it would be unpatriotic to print any of it," Em answered. "Ashton told too much about the inefficiency of the camp, the spoiled food, the lack of sanitation, the measles and typhoid fever that are racing through the troops. And even though Ashton is almost through medical school and could be a real help with the sick, they had put him on kitchen duty. Mr. Rhorer said Charlie's account of the exciting Rough Riders made him better copy."

Alex helped her up the curb. "I hadn't heard about sickness in the camps."

Em sniffed and tossed her head. "No, you wouldn't. They don't put *that* in the newspapers. Papa says there wouldn't be a war if it weren't for the newspapers."

"Isn't Doc for the war?" Alex asked.

Em pushed in a slipping hairpin. "Papa has some very bad memories about the Civil War," she answered. "Two of his older brothers were killed and his father suffered so in a prison camp that he only lived two years after he got home." Em paused as they walked around a sawhorse barricading the sidewalk.

"I wonder when they'll get the new library finished," Alex said as they passed the partially constructed building casting shadows across the blocked sidewalk.

"The last time I talked to Miss Buchanan she said probably not until next year," Em said.

"Grandma says that this town owes a great debt to Jenny Buchanan," Alex commented. "I guess Harper City Library has just about been her whole life. Grandma says she's worked like sixty to get the tax levy approved and the town council behind her to qualify for a Carnegie building. A real go-getter is what Grandma calls her."

"She is that," Em agreed.

Back on the sidewalk, darkened by thick maple foliage, they moved along without speaking. Beyond the site of the new library the houses were set well back from the street. Here and there a lamp shone from an upstairs window where the occupants prepared for bed behind drawn shades. From a few dark houses could be heard the hum of voices and the creak of rocking chairs on front porches.

"Nice to have front-porch weather again," Em said to make conversation. "Mama thinks there's nothing as restful as rocking on the front porch on a summer evening."

"Grandma thinks so too," Alex responded. "I got out our porch chairs for her this morning."

Three blocks beyond, they turned in at the gate leading to the rambling Dudley home. A lamp in a front window cast a beam of light across the broad front porch. Em started up the porch steps. Alex paused.

"Come on," she called back to him.

"Are you sure it isn't too late?" he said.

"Mama will be disappointed if you don't try her cake. It's devil's food."

Alex laughed and mounted the steps. "That's my favorite, Em. Lead me to it."

Inside Em lighted a lamp on the hall table and led the way. She put the lamp on the large table in the middle of the big kitchen. The table was covered with mosquito netting through which could be seen a spoonholder, a vinegar cruet, salt and pepper shakers, a sugar bowl, and a large napkin-covered platter. Em brought the chocolate cake from the pantry.

"Get two saucers, there in the cupboard, will you, Alex?"

Alex put his diploma on the table and brought the dishes.

"Want to eat out on the porch?" Em asked as she took two forks from a drawer.

"Sure, if you want to."

Outside on the dimly lighted front porch, each sat down in a wicker chair.

"Now tell me about yourself, Alex. Here we've been going to the same school for ages and I hardly know you."

"There's not much to tell, Em. I guess I'm an awfully dull fellow. All I know is Dad's business."

"Well, I'd say it's one of the most important businesses in town. What would we do without the Thompson feed store, livery stable, and blacksmith shop? I guess your family business has been there from away back."

"That's right. My great-grandpa started it. He was the town's first blacksmith." Alex paused. "You know, Em, I've been talking to Dad about starting a bicycle shop there next to the feed store," he went on. "Do you think this town needs one?"

"Why, I'd think so. Would you sell or repair them?"

"Both. Quite a few people bring their bicycles to the blacksmith shop to be repaired. Bill Sikes, our blacksmith, really doesn't have time to work on them. Lately I have been doing the repair jobs. Now that I'm through school, Dad wants me to take over all of his bookkeeping. But I figure I could run a bicycle shop and do that too."

Em put their empty dishes on the wicker stand. "Alex, you sound awfully ambitious."

Alex gave a short laugh, uncrossed his knees and leaned forward. "Gee whiz, Em, I don't know when I've talked so much about myself. It's easier to talk to you than I thought it would be."

"Well, of course. After all, I'm just a girl."

"That's just it. Girls kind of scare me. But tonight I made up my mind I was going to walk you home if it was the last thing I ever did."

Em laughed. "Well, Mr. Thompson, now that you've lost your fear of me, why, first thing you know, you'll be squiring all the girls around."

There was a silence. Alex cleared his throat. "No, Em. I'm not interested in *all* girls. I'm just—" At that moment the sound of hoofbeats on the street interrupted.

"That must be Papa," Em said as the horse and buggy turned in and went around toward the barn. The grandfather clock in the hall began to strike.

Alex got to his feet. "Say, that's ten o'clock. I had no idea it was so late. I must go."

Em rose. "Good night, Alex. I wish you good luck with the bicycle shop."

"Thanks." He stopped at the top of the steps. "May I —may I call on you again sometime and talk about it? The bicycle shop, I mean," he stammered slightly.

"Why, I guess so, Alex, if you want to."

"Well, thank you, Em. Good night." He went down the steps and disappeared.

Em peered out into the shadowy front yard. It seemed like midsummer, the night was so warm. A few lightning bugs flickered on and off under the maple tree. On the other side of the walk she could see the faint outline of the iron stag. Once, when she and Ashton were very young, Papa had read aloud the poem about the visit of St. Nicholas. From then on they had called the iron statue Blitzen. How long ago that seemed. Where was Ashton tonight? What was he doing? When would he go to Cuba? She sent out a prayer for his safety.

She heard the back door close and in a few minutes Papa came out, a piece of cake in his hand.

"Still up, Emmy? I thought everyone would be in bed. Someone left the cake out, so I helped myself." The doctor took a bite and sat down.

Em sat near him. "I'm the guilty one. Alex Thompson and I had some."

"Alex? So? Is he going to join the ranks of Emmy Lou admirers?"

"Oh, Papa, you make it sound as though all the boys in town were making a path to our door."

"Well, I remember last summer there was scarcely a night I could find a place to sit here on the front porch. What was that fellow's name who played the mandolin?"

"Dave Emerson. His family moved, remember?"

"Oh, yes. Good thing, too. I can do without his caterwauling this summer." The doctor finished his cake and brushed the crumbs from his trousers. "You looked mighty pretty tonight up on that platform, Emmy. Glad I got to see you get your diploma."

"Me too. You know, Papa, I have to find something to do. Other summers it was fun just to stay at home because there was always school coming along in September. But now, well, time just seems to be stretching out ahead with nothing interesting to fill it."

Dr. Dudley sighed. "Wish you could give me a little of your nothingness time. I'd sit right down and read all the books I never have time for. But I'd think you could find plenty of things to do right here at home."

"You know perfectly well, Papa, that Mama has this house so organized that it runs like a clock. Besides, I can cook and sew fairly well. I'd like to learn something new."

"Would you like to go to normal school and then teach?"

"No. And besides you can't afford it. Ashton has one more year at medical school and Vic may want to go to college."

"That's true. But I could probably manage if you want to go."

"Well, I don't. Very few people in this town even get to high school. They go to work as soon as they graduate from the eighth grade, some even before."

"I know. It makes me shudder to think of children who should be in school or playing outdoors, working out there at the knitting mills or in a factory. There should be a law against it." He got up and walked to the porch rail. Em joined him. He put his arm around her shoulders. "What a nice night. I wonder what Ashton is doing. If it weren't for that crazy war he would be at school becoming what the good Lord meant him to be. And if it hadn't been for that feisty Assistant Secretary of the Navy, Roosevelt, Senator

Lodge, and the dad-ratted newspapers, we wouldn't be in this mess with Spain."

"Papa," Em interrupted. She had to sidetrack his thoughts or he wouldn't sleep a wink he'd get so worked up about the war. "Papa, Alex Thompson is thinking of building a bicycle shop next to their feed store."

"So? Might be a good idea. Everybody and his aunt and uncle seem to be riding wheels these days."

"You know what, Papa?" Em said with sudden inspiration. "I might just try to start a bicycle club here in Harper City. Think I could?"

"Sure thing. Why not? We've got enough other clubs here; literary clubs, music clubs, art clubs, debating societies and the like. At least it would give you something to get your teeth into this summer. By fall you may find something more challenging. You're not old Doc Dudley's daughter for nothing, young lady." He took his arm from her shoulders and tugged briefly at his short beard.

"Hadn't we better go to bed, Papa? It just struck half-past ten."

"'Spect so. Hope the Hefflemans' baby doesn't choose to put in an appearance tonight. I'm tired. Yes, sir, just real tired."

Inside, Em lit a small lamp and mounted the stairs. Papa picked up the other lamp and started back through the hall to the first-floor bedroom he and Mama occupied. Halfway up, Em paused and looked down.

"Good night, Papa," she said softly.

"Good night, daughter. Happy dreams."

Chapter 2

Door to the Future?

Next morning, as usual, Em wakened at six-thirty, but, remembering that she didn't have to get up for school, she closed her eyes and tried to drift off again. The birds in the apple tree outside the open window kept up their early-morning chirpings. A street car clanging along on Fifth Street made further sleep impossible.

She opened her eyes. She knew that at the corner of Main and Fifth the street car would stop to let on the people who went to work at this early hour. Riding through the downtown district, these workers would get off at the farthest edge of town, where, just outside the city limits, the knitting mills, foundry, and glass factory lay.

An hour later those in her own neighborhood who worked downtown would be walking to work; store owners, clerks, stenographers, and bookkeepers, going down to open the businesses and shops at eight o'clock. Among them would be Miss Jenny Buchanan, even though she didn't open the library until nine. Miss Buchanan had a great deal of work to do before she let in the reading public.

Miss Buchanan's stern ways had never scared Em. Ever since the day the librarian had handed Em her first library card, when she was seven, Em had been devoted to her. Miss Buchanan permitted no noise in the library and insisted that books be handled carefully. She gave such scoldings to borrowers late in returning their books that she had little trouble with overdue volumes. The librarian's strict discipline was accepted and obeyed by all without question. It was she who had introduced Em, as a child, to *Sara Crewe* and *Lady Jane*. No wonder Miss Buchanan was one of her favorite people.

Turning on her side, her hand under her cheek, Em looked at the white graduation dress hanging on the closet door. Mama had made it, putting on all the fancy finishing touches by hand. Em thought it her most stylish dress. From the floor-sweeping ruffle at the bottom of the many gored skirt up to the high collar of the bodice it was lovely, lovely, lovely. The sleeves, large shoulder puffs reaching almost to the elbows and fitting tightly to the wrists, were exactly like those on a dress she had seen in the April issue of *Munsey's Magazine,* and *that* dress was worn by an actress, Angela McCaull, playing in New York in *The Heart of Maryland.* The beautiful actress wore a chiffon pom-pom at the back of her high collar. Em had made one for her own dress as nearly like it as possible.

Oh, she *had* felt dressed up last night for sure!

Her new corset hung over a chair back, the corset that, laced tightly, gave her so small a waistline. On the seat of the same chair lay the object that seemed to her a sure sign she was indeed a girl no longer, but a mature woman. It was a bustle she and Mama had purchased last week to wear with the new dress. Worn under her petticoats, it consisted of a belt with a wire protuberance at the rear that held her skirts out in the back and let them fall behind her in a graceful, fashionable sweep to the floor.

Em sighed and stretched her arms over her head. How delightful it had been to walk along, and then, turning suddenly, to hear the back of her skirts swish around on the floor so dramatically that she felt almost like an actress herself.

She threw back the covers, hopped out of bed and stepped to the window. Her room was at the back of the house and she could look out over the long grape arbor that covered the brick walk leading to the red barn on the back of the lot. A chicken yard with a tall wire-meshed fence was adjacent to the barn. A cackling hen told the world that she had laid an egg and her day's work was finished.

On the other side of the barn Em could see Papa's buggy under the open shed. She hoped he had been able to sleep through the night without being called out. Town folk knew that Doc Dudley's bedroom was on the first floor and that they had only to knock at the side door to rouse him to their need.

The clock in the downstairs hall struck seven. Em shooed a fly out the open window and pulled down the sash. Drat the flies, she thought, they were one of the prices one had to pay for summer.

She picked up the pitcher on her washstand and poured water into the china basin. Taking the cake of soap from the soap dish, she lathered a wash cloth and rubbed her face, neck, and ears vigorously. She put on her under-clothes and stockings, then got her high bicycle boots from the closet. She would ride over to Virginia Miller's this morning and tell her about the bicycle club idea.

The tall leather boots laced up to her knees. She tied the laces in a bow and tucked them into the tops. The skirt of her tweed bicycle suit was short, about an inch above her ankles, and so she put on two of her shorter petticoats.

She brushed and combed her brown hair, pulled it back and braided it in a braid that reached below her waist.

She tied a small ribbon bow at the end of the braid and a larger one up at the back of her head. She had found it was better to wear her hair down and not have slipping hairpins to worry about when she was riding her bicycle.

Dressed in a plaid gingham shirtwaist and the skirt, she threw the bed quilt and sheet down over the foot of the brass bed, opened the three windows and left the room to air.

In the kitchen Mama was cutting slices from a side of bacon. "Good morning, Emmy." Mama paused, butcher knife in the air. "You look fresh and pert in that outfit. Where are you off to?"

"Thought I'd ride over to Virginia's this morning to talk about starting a bicycle club. What can I do?" Em glanced at the table, already set for breakfast.

"I wonder if you'd go out and feed the horses before breakfast. Prince and Nick are neighing for their oats. And you might throw some corn to the chickens, too. I want your father to sleep as long as he will this morning. He was out most of the night."

"Where?"

"The Hefflemans'."

"What was it?"

Mama smiled and put down her knife. "Another boy; wouldn't you know it? That makes nine."

"Well, anyway, they have a baseball team now." Em laughed, took a big apron from a hook in the pantry and tied it on before going to the barn.

"Did Alex like the cake?" Mama asked, taking the side of bacon into the pantry.

"Yes, he did. Ate a big piece."

Returning to the kitchen, Mama gave Em a long look. "He's a very nice boy, Em. What time did he leave?"

"At ten o'clock."

"Is he going to call again?"

"Well, he asked if he could."

"What did you tell him?"

"That I guessed so, if he wanted to."

"Em, you should be cordial to that boy. I've known his family for years. His grandma did a fine job of raising him after his mother died. You can just bank on it, he's—"

"I know, Mama. He's dependable. And I *will* be nice to him. Don't worry."

As she walked toward the barn, Em wondered why it was that Mama didn't realize that being dependable was not the only attribute a girl looked for in a man. If a girl thought of him as a possible husband, why *of course* she wanted him dependable, but she also wanted him exciting, and—and—a little dashing. Dependable Alex was, exciting and dashing—never! Now Charlie Hargrove . . . !

By half-past nine Em had finished breakfast, set her own room and Vic's to rights, and dusted the parlor and sitting room. The day was warm. She wouldn't need a jacket. She put a red plaid tam-o-shanter on her head, took her bicycle from the barn and rode off down Main Street.

There was something about riding a bicycle that made her feel like a bird. Feet off the ground, the air rushing by her cheeks, and houses slipping by so fast, oh, it was good! Yes, sir! Flying must be almost like this.

Workmen were hard at it on the new library building. She could hear pounding and sawing as she went by. It reminded her that the library books were due today. She'd go to the library this afternoon.

In the business district she guided her bicycle around and between delivery wagons, buggies, and carriages. Occasionally a horse would toss its head and shy, its driver giving the tam-o-shantered cyclist a dark look. A year ago, when she first got her wheel, she had been afraid to ride downtown on the busy streets, but now she thought nothing of it. She felt thoroughly in command of this flying machine of hers.

On Hickory Street, the other side of town, she found Virginia with broom and soapsuds, vigorously scrubbing the Millers' side porch. Em hopped off at the curb and leaned her bicycle against a maple tree.

"Hard at it, aren't you?" she called as she went up the walk at the side of the house.

"I sure am," Virginia agreed. "It was Lolly's turn to feed the chickens this morning. And didn't she leave the chicken yard gate open and all the chickens got out! We had an awful time catching them. And when we finally got them back in I discovered they had dirtied this porch. Just a minute and I'll be through."

Em walked across the grassy yard to the wooden lawn swing and sat on one side. She pushed slightly on the wooden-slatted floor with her feet and the swing moved back and forth with rhythmic squeaks.

Virginia finished her job, took the bucket and broom around to the back porch, then went to the swing and sat opposite Em. "Well, tell me about Alex Thompson," she said. "I saw him walking you home last night."

Em hesitated, pulled off her tam-o-shanter and straightened her hair ribbon. "Yes, he did. You know, Ginny, he's quite nice. Not extraordinary, but very nice. I want to invite him the next time I have a party, and I want you to be nice to him. But I didn't come over here to talk about Alex. What would you think of organizing a bicycle club this summer?"

"Might be fun. What do you do in a bicycle club besides ride bicycles?" Virginia asked.

"Oh, I don't know exactly, but I think you would plan special trips for the group, ride places together, go on picnics and the like. We might even be able to do something in the way of service for the town," Em added virtuously.

"Let's just start out by being a for-fun club. We'll probably get more girls interested if we do," Virginia stated honestly. "Couldn't we have boys as members, too?"

"If we did then we'd have to have a chaperone every time we went on a trip," Em answered.

"Wouldn't it be a good idea to have boys along in case a bicycle needed fixing?"

"I suppose so. Speaking of fixing bicycles, Alex says he's going to build a bicycle shop next to his father's business." Em leaned her head back against the swing's wooden slats and looked up through the branches of the oak tree that shaded the Millers' side yard.

"He is?" Virginia laughed. "Then I'd say Alex should be a charter member of our club if he's that interested in bicycles."

"Well, frankly, I doubt if he'll really build the shop. He says he's going to join the army as soon as his birthday comes along in the fall."

"Yes? But he'll be too late to get in the Rough Riders' regiment. Don't Charlie Hargrove's letters make the Rough Riders sound brave and dashing? If I were a man I'd want to be on my way to Cuba right now! Wouldn't you?"

"I'm not sure. Ashton's letters aren't so glowing. The food is horrible in his camp and there's a lot of sickness. He says they have been issued only woolen, winter uniforms that are awfully hot even now; what will they be when his regiment gets down to Cuba, where the climate is so much hotter?" Em shook her head thoughtfully.

Virginia shrugged. "Oh, well, I suppose you can't have a war without some discomfort. But just think, Em, by fighting Spain, we are getting to be a real world power. At least that's what Papa says."

"My papa says that no war at all would have been better," Em said sharply.

"Well, I think your father is a wonderful doctor, cured me of lots of things, but he shouldn't be making such unpatriotic remarks. Has he forgotten the *Maine,* blown up right there in Havana harbor last February?"

Em bit her lip. "Of course not. But Papa says there was no proof that the Spanish blew up that ship. He says he wouldn't be surprised if some of those newspaper fellows hadn't had a hand in it, so they'd have something exciting to write about."

"Em Dudley! How can you repeat such a thing?" Virginia stopped the movement of the swing. "I never heard of anything so foolish and unpatriotic."

Em stood up and stepped out of the swing. "Is any of your family in the army?"

"Well, no."

"Then who is calling whom unpatriotic, I'd like to know? My brother Ashton *is!* So if Papa wants to criticize the war I guess he has the right to. His son is in it!" Em's eyes flashed angrily as she started toward the brick walk.

"Oh, Em, come back. I'm sorry. I forgot about Ashton for a minute. Let's talk about something else," Virginia pleaded. "I'll get pencil and paper and we can make a list of girls who might like to join a bicycle club."

That afternoon at two, dressed in a pale green lawn dress, Em, a basket of library books on her arm, walked downtown to the library. As far back as she could remember the Harper City Public Library had been housed in the corner of the Harper building on the downtown square. Old J. D. Harper had stipulated in his will that this space was to be used as a library until such a time as the city should see fit to build an entire building devoted to the housing of the book collection.

Now, thanks to the country's foremost millionaire, Andrew Carnegie, the town was getting a beautiful new library. High time, too, Em thought, with books bursting the seams of the place down on the square.

Six years ago, during the summer, Miss Buchanan had gone to a library school in Chicago. The ladies of the Browning Society had taken turns keeping the library open while she was gone. When she came back, Em could remember the furor in the library as Miss Buchanan, full of her new learning, rearranged all the books according to something she called the Dewey Decimal System, marking the back of each book with numbers and letters.

Many older library patrons complained that they couldn't make head or tail of it, couldn't find the books they wanted, and wished Jenny Buchanan hadn't been so quick to take on such new-fangled foolishness.

Em would never forget the rainy summer morning that the librarian had taken the time to explain to her how the system worked. She had even shown Em the big accession book in which the name and author of each book was entered, and where every book was given a number of its own and placed on the shelves in its proper numerical classification.

The door to the library stood open, letting a shaft of sunlight fall across the floor. Inside, Em blinked in the dim, cool, quiet room. Toward the back, two women stood looking at the novels shelved from floor to ceiling. A small stepladder was nearby to assist readers who wanted those out of reach. At the small table in a back corner, the children's corner, two little girls slowly turned pages of picture books, looking intently at each picture. Nearby, on the floor, an older boy sat cross-legged, lost in the pages of adventure opened on his lap.

At the right of the front door was Miss Buchanan's desk. On top, lined up neatly, little file boxes held the cards taken from the books in circulation. Behind this charging desk stood a big work table. Here Miss Buchanan did her special library tasks, the cataloguing of new books and the mending of old ones. It was well known that Jenny Buchanan lived, breathed, and dreamed "library."

Em watched the librarian for a moment before going to the desk to return the books. Miss Buchanan's head was bent over the big accession book in which she wrote. Her gray hair was fastened in a big round twist on top of her head; a tortoise shell comb neatly held up the back hair. The high starched collar of her blue shirtwaist was softened by a black ribbon bow under her chin.

Em walked toward the desk. The librarian looked up and smiled. She put down her pen, took the pince-nez spectacles from her nose, gave a slight pull on their chain and they sprang up to the gold button pinned below the shoulder of her shirtwaist. Em knew if she lived to a ripe old age she would never cease to be entranced at this act of Miss Buchanan's—making her glasses repose just above her ample bosom, the chain disappearing as if by magic. When she was a little girl, this phenomenon had been a part of the thrill of a visit to the library.

Standing behind the desk, the librarian took Em's books. "I saw you graduate last night, Emmy Lou." She still addressed Em by her childhood nickname, the one she had shortened when she started to high school. "It was a nice affair. I was proud of every one of the graduates. It seems only yesterday that I was giving them Palmer Cox's *Brownies* and Kate Greenaway's *Marigold Garden*. How is your mother?"

"Very well, thank you."

The librarian took the proper card from the file and put it in the book pocket. "Did she like this, *The Spirit of Sweetwater?*"

"Yes, she did, and we all loved *The Prisoner of Zenda.*"

"Everyone does. A sequel to it is running as a serial in *McClure's Magazine.* It is called *Rupert of Hentzau.* I expect it will be out in book form soon."

"Oh, I'll want to read that!" Em exclaimed. "I kept wondering what happened next to Queen Flavia and Rudolf Rassendyll. What do you suggest I take for Papa?"

"Well, Maylen likes something with meat on its bones. How about the book I just catalogued, *The Life and Character of U. S. Grant* by Hamlin Garland?" Miss Buchanan took the book from the table. "You go on and select the rest of your books and I'll paste a pocket in this one."

Years ago, Miss Buchanan had gone to school with Papa. She always called him Maylen. Sometimes Em wondered if there hadn't been a hint of romance between them before Papa went off to Rush Medical School and met Mama in Chicago.

Em joined the ladies in front of the fiction shelves. Now, what should she get for Mama, who liked lots of romance? After some browsing, Em chose *The Red Hill Tragedy* by Mrs. Southworth and *The Fair God* by Lew Wallace for Mama; Mama had loved his *Ben Hur.* Papa might want to read *The Fair God* also, he admired General Wallace so much. In fact, everyone in Indiana was proud that this well-known author was a Hoosier.

For herself she took a new book by S. Weir Mitchell, *Hugh Wynne.* She had read someplace that the author was a physician like Papa. She read his books with added pleasure. She wondered how a doctor ever found time to write a book. Certainly Papa had no free time for such a thing.

She always selected Vic's book last. It was so pleasant to browse among the books in the children's corner. On the shelves the volumes from Alcott to Yonge seemed like real friends. She had read so many of them more than once. Vic had asked for another by Henty; soon he would have read all by this author. She pulled *Under Drake's Flag* from the shelf. Papa once said that he thought reading the Henty books was as good as a course in History. Mr. Henty was a war correspondent for the London *Standard,* Papa said, and knew history firsthand.

At the desk Miss Buchanan charged Em's books, stamping all the Dudleys' library cards with the due dates.

"Emmy Lou, what are you going to do now that you have finished school?" she asked.

Em placed the books in her basket. "I really don't know. Virginia Miller and I thought we might start a bicycle club."

"I'm going to need some help when the new library building is ready. What about you? Would you be interested in a job?" The librarian looked up at Em.

Em set her basket on the desk. "Me, work in the library? Why, I never thought of it. I don't think I know enough."

"You could learn. You certainly have been a reader all your life. Knowing books is important. The job will pay twenty dollars a month."

Em's hand tightened on the basket handle. What a lot of money for working in such an interesting place as a library! Money of her own! And in that grand new building, too!

"I'll talk to Mama and Papa about it," she said slowly. "Do you really think I could do it, Miss Buchanan?"

"Wouldn't have asked you if I had thought otherwise," the librarian returned tartly. "I've known you all your life. As I look at it, you have a good education, your mother has brought you up right, and—you are Doc Dudley's daughter."

Walking home under the shade of Main Street's maples, Em scarcely noticed the weight of the basket. Her mind was busy picturing herself in the new library, ingratiating Harper City library patrons with her knowledge and charm.

At the site of the new library she paused and looked up the many steps leading to the big front doors. Were they the doors to her future? Until now her dreams of the future had been centered upon a handsome man proposing marriage and a church wedding with herself in a beautiful bridal gown. She had never daydreamed beyond the wedding, the rest being only a rosy haze.

No proposal had materialized. She would be eighteen in October. Maybe she was going to be a spinster like Miss Buchanan. Perhaps she *should* take this position. She didn't want to be twiddling her thumbs for years and years.

She put the basket in her other hand and sauntered dreamily home.

Chapter 3

The H.C.B.C.

In the days that followed the library job was discussed pro and con by all members of the family.

Vic was all for it. "Gee, Sis, you could get me a book every day if I wanted it!" he exclaimed.

Mama thought it would be just wonderful to be where one could read books all the time. Papa said he thought there was more to working in a library than just reading books, and he wasn't sure he wanted Em to work. People would think he couldn't support his women folk.

Mama said, "Maylen, don't be so old-fashioned. Lots of girls are taking jobs these days and not just the ones whose fathers can't support them, either. I say let Emmy decide. There's no one I'd rather have her work for than Jenny Buchanan."

"Yes, Jenny is a fine woman," Papa agreed. "When would you have to start?" He looked at Em.

"I don't know. Probably when the new building is finished. I expect that will be sometime after the first of the year."

"Well, by that time you may find you have plenty to do around home here. And I could use some help down at my office on busy days, especially Saturday afternoons when the farmers come to town." Dr. Dudley looked thoughtful. "It will sure be fine when Ashton gets his degree and joins me. I've been thinking I'd rent that room next to my office when he does. It would be nice to give him an examination room all his own. Plague take that war, anyway, taking a valuable boy like Ashton and wasting his talents on potato peeling."

"Papa, you know I'm not much good in your office," Em said. "About all I can do is help some with the crying babies in the waiting room."

"Well, that's quite a help to me when several of them start bawling at the same time."

On Wednesday afternoon, June 1, seven bicycles lay on the front lawn at the Dudleys'. On the porch eight girls chattered and laughed gaily, all talking at once, making so much noise that the Dudleys' dog, Handsome, lying under the maple tree, stirred from his nap and retreated to the back yard to finish his sleep beneath the shade of the grape arbor.

Virginia Miller stood up. "Listen girls. We're not here to talk but to organize a bicycle club. We'll have to come to order." The girls stopped talking and looked at her expectantly. "First off, I expect we should elect officers. Don't you think so?"

"I nominate Virginia Miller for president since this is her idea," Lucile Jackson said from the top porch step.

"No, it was Em's idea," Virginia confessed. "She should be president."

"I couldn't possibly be president," Em said quickly. "I just might be doing something very important soon. I wouldn't have time to run a club."

Lucile turned to Em. "Now what could be more important than a club? I'd like to know. Don't be so mysterious, Em. What is it?"

"I'd rather not say until it's definite." Em looked around at the interested faces, enjoying the expressions of curiosity.

"I bet I know! Em's going to get married. Oh, who is it, Em? When is the wedding and aren't you ashamed, not telling us?" Dottie Leghorn burst in excitedly.

Em laughed. "Dottie, what an idea! Of course that's not it. You know very well no man has been courting me."

"Well, I've seen several walking home with you before school was out," Dottie pursued the subject.

"That's just it," Em returned, "several, but no special one."

By this time Virginia had sat down. She leaned forward and said in a lowered voice, "Did you know, girls, that Alex Thompson walked Em home last Friday, after graduation?"

Madge Swanson gave a squeal. "Emmy, he didn't! That old sobersides! Did he ever say anything? What did you talk about?"

"Now, don't make fun of him," Em defended Alex. "He is very nice. He may start a bicycle shop. Think how handy that would be for all of you when something goes wrong with your wheel."

Virginia stood up again. "Girls, we came here to organize a bicycle club, not to talk about Em's beaux."

"I move we make Virginia president, unanimously," Em said.

"Second the motion," Dottie said quickly.

Before Virginia could say a word, Em cut in, "It's moved and seconded that Virginia be president. All in favor say aye." From every mouth but Virginia's came an "aye."

"There, Ginny, you're president." Em grinned up at her.

"Well, thank you all for your confidence in me," Virginia said, straightening her shoulders and lifting her head to suit the dignity of her new office.

"Oh, don't flatter yourself, Gin," Molly Flannery said. "The rest of us are too lazy to be president. You'll have to do all the work."

Virginia's eyes narrowed slightly. She winked at Em. "Do I hear a nomination for secretary of this club?"

"I move Molly Flannery be made secretary by acclamation," Em answered Virginia's wink.

Before Molly knew it she had been swept into office.

"Now we'll see who does the work! Madam Secretary will you get pencil and paper and take down the minutes of this meeting?" Virginia laughed and made a mock bow to Molly.

Em went inside and brought tablet and pencil for the new secretary.

By half-past three they had elected a treasurer, decided on the amount of dues per month, how often they should meet, and listed the names of other girls who would be prospective members. The name of the club was to be The Harper City Bicycle Club, or, for short, the H.C.B.C.

Molly jabbed her pencil down for the last period. "There, Ginny Miller, I'll not write another line. Em, get out your bicycle and we'll all ride down to the ice cream parlor. Aunt Mamie gave me a dollar for graduation. I'll treat all of you to ice cream."

Em stood up. "Save your money, Molly. Mama made lemonade for us and I baked a cake this morning. Come in with me, Dottie, and help carry things out."

At half-past five Dr. Dudley found Em sweeping cake crumbs from the porch. Putting down his medicine bag, he sat in a rocker and took off his hat. Em leaned the broom against the railing and sat opposite.

"Well, Emmy, did you get your club started?" He rocked slowly.

"Yes. The Harper City Bicycle Club has eight charter members. Ginny Miller is president."

"So? How come they didn't make you president? It was your idea."

"Someone did mention me. But I thought I'd better not take it on, just in case I do work at the library." She leaned forward. "Papa, what do you think? Should I tell Miss Buchanan yes?"

"Well—" The doctor leaned his head against the chair back and paused; a floor board squeaked under the movement of his rocker. "I must say that my pride in providing for my family would suffer somewhat if you worked. But looking at it from your side, I expect you would enjoy it and probably would learn a great deal, not just from the books you would handle but from working under Jenny Buchanan. She's a great person, a real fighter and go-getter. This town could use a lot of Jenny Buchanans to my way of thinking."

"I think I'll stop by tomorrow and tell her that I'll do it. Thanks, Papa." Em stood up. "And I don't think anyone in town will ever question Doc Dudley's ability to care for his family." She ran her fingers through his hair and placed a light kiss upon his forehead.

"There's the paper boy," the doctor announced, pushing back the hair his daughter had set awry.

Em went down the steps and met the *News* carrier. "Hello, Bud," she greeted as the boy took a paper from the heavy bag on his shoulder.

"Hello." He looked up. "Hello, Doc Dudley."

"Hello, Bud. I see you recovered from the measles in great shape. How's your grandma?"

"Just fine, Doc. Those last pills you gave her fixed her up just right."

"Glad to hear it."

Em dropped the paper into her father's lap. He unfolded it and together they stared at the black headline:

ROUGH RIDERS AND TROOPS
GATHER IN TAMPA

"I wonder if Ashton is there too," Em said softly.

The doctor sighed. "I imagine he may be. Oh, Emmy, what I wouldn't give to have that boy back in school where he belongs. This war is ridiculous. Our war department is entirely inadequate. If we win it will be only because Spain's fighting force is even more inadequate than ours."

"You sound sort of unpatriotic, Papa."

"If speaking the truth is unpatriotic then I am." He looked back at the newspaper. "I see there's another letter here from Charlie Hargrove. More flag waving, I suppose. We'll have to wait for a letter from Ashton to get the truth about conditions.

Em went inside to help with supper, leaving her father reading and mumbling complaints to himself. She would read Charlie's letter after supper when Papa had finished with the paper.

Next afternoon Em went to the library. "I've decided I *would* like to work for you, Miss Buchanan," she said, standing in front of the desk.

"Good." The librarian put two books to be mended on the table behind her. "I sort of thought you would. Now the whole thing will have to go through the Library Board, you know. You write a letter to Bert Long, saying you would like to apply for the job. Bert is president of the Library Board. It's just a matter of form, of course; Bert refers all such things to me. I'm going to need two assistants. I've asked Jessie Overstreet if she would like to work in the library. Do you know her?"

"Why, yes. She dropped out of high school last year when her father died."

"That's right. She's been helping her mother with dress-making. There are four younger children. I expect Mrs. Overstreet has a hard time making ends meet. Jessie is a smart girl. A pity she had to quit school. I believe she will do well in the library. I've had my eye on her ever since she was a tiny girl, just as I have you."

Em smiled down at the librarian. "You have watched most of us grow up, haven't you? I expect you know every-one in town."

"Just about. I was wondering, Emmy Lou, if you could spend a couple of mornings a week here with me, so I can give you some instructions. Of course your pay won't start until the new building opens. But once we get in there I won't have much time to give you and Jessie. I'll want you to go ahead and do things on your own then."

Em looked around and wondered what there was she didn't know about this place. Miss Buchanan's job seemed easy, just stamping books to take out and putting cards in those returned. "Why yes, I can come. What days would you like to have me?"

"Suppose you start next week. You come Tuesday and Thursday mornings. If Jessie decides to take the position, I'll take her through the paces on Wednesdays and Fridays."

"What time?"

"I get here at eight o'clock. Can you be here at that time?"

"Certainly."

"Be sure to bring a big apron to protect your dress. When we get in the new building we'll have a janitor, but here, I do the cleaning. You might just as well get used to doing everything as I have through the years."

Walking home, Em thought about the new job. Somehow, she had only pictured herself seated behind the desk, reading a good book, stopping occasionally to stamp a borrower's library card as he took out a book. It had seemed such nice clean work. Wearing an apron suggested a side of this occupation that she had not considered.

In front of the new building she paused; then, lifting her skirts slightly, she crossed the dusty, sidewalk section and mounted the steps. Through the open door she could see men at work. How beautiful it was going to be! From here she could see the lower lobby with its tile floor and marble steps leading up to the main stack room. The charging desk would be up there she supposed. Perhaps later on Miss Buchanan would take her in and show her the whole place.

Imagine, Em Dudley working in the handsome, new Harper City Public Library! She was very lucky to have this opportunity. She would work hard, she vowed; Miss Buchanan must never regret that she had employed Doc Dudley's daughter.

Walking on toward home, she thought of Jessie Overstreet. Jessie should have graduated in the class of '98 too. The Overstreets lived on the other side of town, had moved there right after Mr. Overstreet's death; moved, Em judged, into a house with cheaper rent. If Jessie did take the library position, she went on thinking, she would get to know the girl better. As she remembered, Jessie was dark-haired, tall and very pretty. It was too bad she had had to quit school.

The first thing next morning, Em wrote a letter to the president of the Library Board, then rode her bicycle to the post office to mail it. Afterward she went on to the

Millers' to tell Virginia about the position in the new library that was soon to be hers. Virginia's plans for the bicycle club had to play second fiddle to Em's announcement.

The headlines in the newspaper on the following Monday evening, June 6, stated:

COMMANDER MCCALLA SEIZES
LOWER BAY AT GUANTANAMO

At the supper table Papa put the paper beside his plate, glancing at it between bites. "I don't know what good it's going to do the Navy to take a bay if they don't have any troops on land. Where in tarnation are those Rough Riders Teddy Roosevelt's been training. From the build-up the newspapers have given them, the Spaniards will just fade away at the sight of them."

"I guess they must still be in Tampa getting ready to go to Cuba," Em said, buttering a hot biscuit. "Just think of the ships they'll have to have there to carry all those men across. And there'll be horses, too, won't there?"

"That's right. The Rough Riders are a cavalry outfit. You wouldn't catch that Roosevelt training anything as slow as infantry." The doctor took the dish of potatoes Em passed him.

"Maylen, why do you have such a poor opinion of Colonel Roosevelt? He seems to me to be a fine man. He's very energetic and gets things done." Mama went to the kitchen and came back with the coffee pot.

"Well, maybe I am hard on the man," the doctor conceded. "But I don't believe President McKinley would have got us into this war if it hadn't been for Roosevelt and Senator Lodge. With those two in Washington waving the flag and beating the drum, so to speak, and the newspapers embroidering their stories with little regard for facts—well, we're into it now up to our necks. I just hope we get out in one piece."

"Now eat your supper, Maylen. Getting yourself so worked up can't be good for your digestion," Mama admonished. She turned to Em. "It's tomorrow you start your training with Miss Buchanan, isn't it?"

"Yes. I want to be there before eight. Will you wake me when you get up? I must be on time."

"I'd like another piece of meat, please," Vic said, passing his plate. "Em, I finished my book. Will you take it back and bring me another?"

"Sure." Em took the plate and put a pork chop on it. "I don't mind selecting books for you. But I think you should go to the library yourself sometimes and do your own choosing. That's half the fun."

"I will when the new library opens." Vic took back his plate and flooded the valleys in his mashed potatoes with gravy. "There are always too many little kids there in that corner where my books are. Makes me feel like a baby."

"Victor, don't say kids. The word is children," Mama corrected.

"Yes, ma'am."

"Nellie, would you bring me my pie, now?" the doctor asked. "I've got to get down to the office for my evening hours, you know."

"Certainly, Maylen." Mama took Papa's plate to the kitchen, returned with the pie and was just setting it in front of him when there was a loud knock at the front door.

"Doc! Doc Dudley!" an excited voice called out.

"Now wouldn't you know it? No dessert again!" Dr. Dudley hastily wiped his mouth and beard with his napkin, rose and strode quickly through the hall, Em and Vic following.

"Doc, it's my boy, Jimmy. He fell out of a cherry tree and I think he broke his leg," the man at the door said.

"I'll be right there, Amos, as soon as I hitch up. You go on back and don't move him whatever you do." The doctor took his hat from the hall tree and picked up his bag. Em and Vic were already out the kitchen door making for the barn to help hitch up. They knew Amos Barney lived in the country; Papa couldn't waste a minute.

As he climbed into the buggy, the doctor said, "Emmy, you go down to the office and stay there till I get back so you can tell the folks I had an emergency call. I'll be there as soon as I set Jimmy's leg."

"All right, Papa."

Vic and Em watched their father crack the whip over Prince's head, alerting the horse to the need for speed. They saw the rig disappear around the house and heard the quick staccato of the horse's hoofs on the brick street. Prince, Papa had once said, should have an M.D. after his name too, his speed contributed so much to doctoring. Getting places in a hurry was imperative.

"I don't see why Ashton wants to be a doctor," Vic said. "One thing sure, I'm not going to be one. It seems like Papa never gets to finish a meal."

"Oh, he can eat that pie when he gets home," Em returned. "Come on. Let's go back and eat ours. What *do* you want to be, Vic?"

"A soldier or a fireman, or maybe an explorer. I don't know which." He reached down and stroked Handsome's head as the dog joined them under the grape arbor.

"Well, you have plenty of time to decide. But being a doctor is just about the most important and most helpful thing you could be. Harper City couldn't get along without Papa."

"Oh, I know that." Vic held the back door open for his sister and Handsome. "But I wouldn't like missing my pie the way he has to."

Chapter 4

All's Right

It was half-past seven next morning when Em left the house. The day was going to be hot, she thought, as she tucked under her arm the newspaper package containing her apron. It was pleasant enough on the sidewalk under the shade trees, but, even this early, crossing the streets where one got the full blast of morning sun, it was scorching.

Rose bushes were beginning to bloom, she noticed. Some of the ramblers climbing over fences were so full of bright red flowers she could scarcely see the pickets. She wished she had taken time to look at the bush in the back yard at home. It would have been nice to have brought a bouquet for Miss Buchanan. But she had been so eager to arrive on time.

The hands on the Court House clock showed ten minutes to eight when she arrived at the library. The door was locked and the shades down. She had beat Miss Buchanan! Oh, well, she didn't mind. Much better to be ten minutes early than one minute late.

She sauntered slowly to Iseley's Big Store next door and looked at the merchandise displayed in the show windows. One window was full of gray granite dishpans. A big sign stated that these would go on sale for five cents apiece at eleven this morning. What a bargain! She wondered if Mama knew about this sale. The window beyond was filled with yard goods, the bolts arranged so that portions of material hung down in graceful festoons. There was printed calico, checked gingham, flowered lawn, plain dimity, and shiny satin. She had never had a satin dress. Maybe when she started earning money at her new job she could have one.

"Good morning, Em."

She turned from the window and saw that Alex Thompson had stopped his bicycle at the edge of the sidewalk.

"Good morning, Alex." She walked toward him.

"Aren't you downtown kind of early?"

"I'm waiting for Miss Buchanan to open the library. She's going to teach me how she does things. When the new library opens I'm going to work there. Do you usually get downtown this early?"

Alex took off his cap and wiped his forehead with a handkerchief. "It's usually earlier, around seven. But this morning I weeded Grandma's garden. It's hard for her to get down on her knees to do it." He put the handkerchief in his pocket and returned the cap to his head. "So, you're going to be a librarian. That'll be fine. The new building is going to be mighty grand."

Em's pulse quickened as he applied the word *librarian* to her. Somehow she hadn't thought of the word being used in reference to Em Dudley. She had thought of the new job only as being a helper for Miss Buchanan. But why couldn't she call herself a librarian if she worked in the library? It seemed logical. She gave Alex a warm smile. "Yes, I *am* going to be a librarian."

"I'll have to start taking books again." Alex smiled and leaned back on the bicycle seat, one foot on the curb.

"Would you mind if I called on you at home sometime, Em?"

"Why—no, I wouldn't mind." Em looked at him from under the broad brim of her straw hat. "Do you still plan to build that bicycle shop?"

"Yes, I do. Dad says we'll start digging the cellar in a week or so. Should have it ready to open by fall."

"That's good. Some of us girls started a bicycle club last week." At that moment the Court House clock began to strike. "Oh, my goodness, I've got to go. And I wanted to be early. Good-bye, Alex."

"Good-bye, Em." He tipped his cap and watched her disappear through the library door which had just been unlocked by the punctual Miss Buchanan. He adjusted the bicycle clamps around his trousers at the ankles and pedaled away.

Before the morning was an hour old, Em discovered why she had been told to bring an apron. Under Miss Buchanan's direction, she lightly sprinkled water over the floor, then swept with a heavy broom. Never had the library seemed so big! By the time she got all the dirt swept into a pile outside the front door, the first patrons began arriving. The sun beat down on her with strong, hot rays as she brushed the dirt across the sidewalk toward the curb. The dirt in the gutter, she took the clean handkerchief from her apron pocket and wiped her damp face. Returning it, very dirty, to her pocket, she looked ruefully at her hands. One blister in the palm of one and two in the other had swollen into small white mounds of pain.

Inside again, she returned the broom to its corner in the back storeroom and got busy with a dust cloth. The furniture, the window sills, the tops of all the books, and the bare portions of the shelves must be gone over everyday, Miss Buchanan told her. "Perhaps it won't be so dirty in the new building. There we won't have an un-paved street running alongside as we do here." Harper City's Main Street was brick, but all others were unpaved. Trying to keep their homes dusted, caused housekeepers no end of work. Em began to appreciate the fact that her house was in the middle of a block on Main Street. She had never seen so much dust on things before.

At half-past ten, Miss Buchanan had Em sit at a table in the back room, then explained how she wanted pockets and printed library-rules-and-regulations slips pasted in several stacks of books. They were not new ones, but a gift from a library patron, the librarian told Em. When-ever anyone in Harper City cleaned his attic, Miss Bu-chanan went on, the library usually got some books. Some, of course, were trash and had to be discarded, but quite often attics provided real treasures for the library.

There was a fourteen-inch-square piece of marble on the table. Holding the pockets and rules slips in place on the marble slab, Em daubed the backs with paste, using a small varnish brush for the operation. Miss Buchanan said she made this paste herself. Em wondered what she put in it; it smelled awful.

Soon the tips of Em's fingers were crusty with dried paste. Her eyes watered and her nose itched. It must be the strong odor of the paste, she decided. She rubbed her eyes and scratched her nose with the back of her hand. She didn't want to take time to wash off the paste until she had finished the job.

The books, she noted, were in good condition, but awfully dusty. She had to dust each one before pasting. There was a set of Dickens and another by Anthony Trollope besides many individual titles. She pasted the two sets quickly, not stopping to look inside even one.

The Dudleys had sets of Dickens and Trollope at home.

The two sets completed and stacked neatly at the far end of the table, she began on the others. Now, the temptation to dip into each book began to slow her progress. Here was a copy of Bellamy's *Looking Backward*. She had heard of it and had read someplace that it was a story of Utopia. She should read it. A librarian should know every book, she supposed, or at least as many as she could manage.

Oh, look here! Now how do you suppose this fairly new book got with this bunch of old ones? It was *Titus, a Comrade of the Cross*. In a recent magazine she had read an interview with the author, Florence Morse Kingsley. The article had stated that the book had sold over a million copies in the last three years and had been translated into Swedish, German, Spanish and Japanese. Imagine being able to write a book good enough to deserve all that! Em opened the book to the first chapter and read the first paragraph.

Six pages later, a rustle at the door caused her to look up. Miss Buchanan smiled as Em guiltily closed the book and picked up a pocket.

"How is it going?"

"All right. I'm afraid I got into this book and forgot where I was," Em explained, dipping the brush into the paste jar.

"That's all right. How can you recommend a book if you don't know what's inside?" The librarian picked up the book and glanced at the title page. "This one is well nigh as popular as *Ben Hur*, and the author is a woman," she added.

"I know. You just wonder how a woman would know enough to write such a book." Em took back the volume and pasted a pocket in the front.

"She was fortunate in being brought up in a home with many books," the librarian said, "and also, she is a graduate of Wellesley College."

"Well, I could never write a book no matter how many colleges I went to or how many books I had read."

Miss Buchanan laughed. "Well, don't let it worry you. Just remember that no author would have much of an audience if it weren't for librarians handing out their brain children to the public. I think you better put things away here. It's almost twelve o'clock. I close from twelve until two, you know."

Em looked at her watch. "Why, so it is. This morning has just flown." She looked at the remaining books. "I'm sorry I didn't finish these. It is such a temptation to dip in here and there."

"That's all right. Jessie is coming in tomorrow and I shall want her to learn this phase of the work too."

Together, Miss Buchanan and Em walked along Main Street. When they passed the new library building, Em said, "I'd love to see the inside sometime. Do you suppose I could?"

"I'll take you through myself. I can't today. Mother had a headache this morning and I want to get home to her. How about tomorrow a little after twelve? I'll bring Jessie and the three of us can go in and see how things are progressing."

"I'll meet you here," Em promised.

At home, Em found the family at the dinner table. The doctor usually made house calls in the morning, trying to get home promptly at twelve so that he would have time for a short nap after dinner before going to his office at two. This daytime rest period was important; his sleep at night was so often interrupted.

Em slipped into her place. Mama passed the food and by the time Em's plate was filled, she was telling the family about her morning in the library. So engrossed was she in the tale that she failed to notice the unopened letter beside the doctor's water glass.

At last Vic broke in. "Can't you hurry and eat, Em, so Papa can read us Ashton's letter?"

Em put down her fork. "Oh, did we get a letter? Read it, Papa, don't wait for me to finish."

The doctor took a sip of coffee and picked up the letter. "It's from Tampa," he stated, looking at the postmark. He tore an end of the envelope and pulled out the pages covered with fine, legible handwriting.

Mama once said that if Ashton hadn't decided to be a doctor he could have become a writer; he was so good at describing things on paper. Ever since he had left for college the family had made a big thing of his letters, never opening them until the entire family was present.

Em put her hands in her lap as Papa cleared his throat and began to read.

Dear People on Main Street,
Here I am in Tampa, along with thousands of United States regulars and volunteers. I have never seen such confusion in all my life. If any of us ever get to Cuba, it will be a miracle.

We are loading the ships in port with supplies; six months rations for twenty thousand men—quite a job, especially in 100-degree temperature and all of us wearing winter uniforms.

General Shafter is in charge. This extreme heat is doubly hard on him. He weighs at least 300 pounds and he rides around in a buggy trying to bring order to the chaos. I guess there is no horse strong enough to carry him on its back.

It is nine miles from Tampa to the port; a one-track railroad connects the two. They say there are over 300 cars loaded with war material in Tampa, but since the invoices and bills of lad-ing have not been received, the officers have had to break open freight car seals and hunt from car to car to find out whether they contain clothing, grain, ammunition, guns, or horse equipment. What a mess!

I talked to a newspaperman last night. He said it looks like old home week in Tampa. The rocking chairs on the porches of the winter hotels are kept in motion by officers who haven't seen one another since West Point days. Glad this war is good for something. Personally I am more than a little disenchanted with the whole thing.

Speaking of newspapermen, they are everywhere. This should be the best reported war of all times. I met one the other day, such a fine young fellow, who asked me a great many questions. So I asked him his name. It was Crane, Stephen Crane. I told him that his name seemed very familiar to me. Then he said maybe I had read his book. Remember *The Red Badge of Courage*, Papa, that story of the Civil War that you said was the real thing? Well, he wrote it.

The doctor looked up. "Well, can you beat that! Ashton meeting that fellow! His book is worth a dozen of the other mealy-mouthed tales authors turned out about the Civil War."

Em made a mental note to look up that book. Imagine, Ashton meeting a real author!

The doctor resumed.

General Fitzhugh Lee is in charge of the Seventh Corps of volunteers. I've learned that he is the nephew of Robert E. Lee. He does not seem to have inherited any of his uncle's military genius; at any rate he has done nothing to relieve the chaotic state of this concentration of troops.

Very much in evidence are the famous Rough Riders and their officers, Colonel Wood and Lieutenant Colonel Roosevelt. If there is any order at all here, it is with that troop. They got their tents up in jig time and have been drilling regularly on foot and on horseback. I heard that there are not enough troopships to take their horses to Cuba, so the Rough Riders will be afoot the same as the rest of us.

Colonel Roosevelt is an interesting-looking man. Hands on hips, dressed in the light brown uniform of the Rough Riders, his hat rolled up on one side, he peers out from behind his nose glasses, disapproving the complete disorder of most of this site. But on occasion his mustached, toothy grin lights up his expressive face and one feels drawn to him. He has great personal magnetism.

I have looked everywhere for Charlie Hargrove. I hope he isn't laid up with typhoid or malaria as so many are. The tropical heat here is a handicap. Being a medical student, I worry about yellow fever, sure to be prevalent in Cuba.

It is evening now, and a little cooler. I must draw this to a close and try to sleep. I think we will be leaving for Cuba in a few days. I'll write again as soon as I can manage it.

> *Love to all,*
> Ashton

The doctor folded the sheets and put them back in the envelope. Em resumed eating, wondering if Charlie Hargrove *did* have malaria.

"I didn't know war was like that," Vic said. "I thought Ashton would be charging on the enemy by this time instead of loading ships."

"Son, war is just plain misery from beginning to end even when the cause is right. Back in '61 we fought to save our Union. I believe that was a just cause. But in this one, it seems to me, we're just butting in where we've no right to be. If it serves any purpose at all, it will be to show the War Department how inadequate our fighting force is. That Secretary of War, Alger, hasn't done anything but twiddle his thumbs ever since President McKinley appointed him."

Em went to the kitchen and returned with the coffee pot. "How about some more coffee, Papa?"

"Yes, please, Em." The doctor held up his cup. "We must all write letters to Ashton. That's the least we can do. But it's a moot question as to whether mail will ever reach him; that whole operation is so disorganized." He finished his coffee. "Will you excuse me? I'm going to lie down for a spell." He folded his napkin, rolled it, put it in his napkin ring and rose. "Em, now that you're working at the library, I suppose you'll always be late to dinner."

"I expect so, Papa. At least on Tuesdays and Thursdays until the new building is ready. Then it will be every day." Em pushed her plate aside and pulled her piece of cherry pie toward her. "I think I'll wait until tomorrow to write to Ashton, after I have gone through the new library. I know he'll be interested in how it's coming along."

"I'll be interested myself," Mama said, stirring the sugar in her coffee.

"Bert Long was in the office yesterday to get some medicine for his mother. He said they are planning a very fancy program for the library opening." Papa looked at Em. "You should be proud, Emmy, to be a part of that institution. It's going to be the biggest educational and recreational asset Harper City ever acquired. I've never been much of an admirer of Andrew Carnegie. It seems to me that he so often made his money by questionable means. Still, you have to give the devil his due. The Carnegie libraries he has pledged to the country will probably be the biggest step forward in education the United States will ever know."

Em swallowed a bite of pie and put down her fork. "Did Mr. Long say anything about my letter to him?"

"Yes. He said Jenny Buchanan recommended you highly, also Jessie Overstreet. You'll probably get a letter confirming your appointment after the next meeting of the Library Board."

"Maylen, you better run along and take your nap." Mama

began stacking the dishes. "Victor, did you pull the shades in the sitting room for Papa's nap as I told you?"

"Yes, Mama. May I go fishing with Terry Higgins? We dug our worms this morning."

"Where do you intend to fish?"

"At the end of Grant Street, just below the dam."

"All right. But get back in time to clean up before supper."

Papa and Vic left the room. Mama carried some dishes to the kitchen, returned and sat at the table. Em ate slowly.

"I was just thinking, Emmy Lou," Mama said, "of the day you got your first library card. Remember?" Em nodded. "If you had known then that the day would come when you would be working in the library, well, I expect you would just have exploded with joy."

"Honestly, Mama, I feel sort of like an explosion right now. And I'm scared, too, there's so much I don't know. There is a lot more to working in a library than just liking to read."

Her pie finished, Em helped carry the rest of the dishes to the kitchen. Mama, sleeves rolled high, put the glasses in the dishpan of soapy water.

"Ready for me to take out the garbage?" Em asked.

"Yes, it's all on that plate. Throw those bread crusts on top to the chickens."

Em walked under the cool grape arbor toward the back of the lot. She tossed the bread to the hens and emptied the rest into the big lard can back of the barn.

The hot sun, the low contented clucks of the hens, the occasional neighs and stomps of Prince and Nick in their stalls, the whistle of a cardinal in the apple tree, and the mournful cooing of doves on top of the barn gave her contentment.

If only Ashton were comfortable and Charlie Hargrove

all right, she thought, everything in her world would be wonderful.

She was seventeen, through school, and had a job in a building that was as nearly like a palace as she'd ever seen. Of course there was no prince or knight on the horizon. Certainly Alex Thompson bore no resemblance to either, and Charlie probably didn't even remember her. But surely one would come along in time.

She returned slowly under the grape arbor, murmuring:

> "God's in His Heaven,
> All's right with the world!"

At least it was, in her world, Harper City.

Chapter 5

A Philanthropic Purpose

In order to keep the appointment at the new library next day, Em ate her dinner early. The twelve o'clock whistle blew as she reached the site. The workmen, seated outside on the front steps, were eating from tin lunch pails.

As she waited on the sidewalk, Em looked up at the second-story windows, wondering to what use the upstairs would be put. Shortly Miss Buchanan and a tall young woman arrived from downtown. Em had not seen Jessie Overstreet for more than a year.

"Have you been waiting long, Emmy Lou?" Miss Buchanan asked.

"Just a few minutes. Hello, Jessie. It's been such a long time since I saw you." Em hadn't remembered that Jessie was so beautiful.

"Hello, Em. It *has* been a long while," Jessie agreed. "But I guess we'll be seeing a lot of one another when the new library opens."

"Well, come on, girls, let's go in." The librarian led the way. One of the men on the steps rose as they approached. "Good afternoon, Joe," she greeted him. "How are things progressing?"

"According to schedule, Miss Buchanan. We'll have the doors and windows and furnace in by cold weather. The inside should be finished shortly after that." The man set his hat on the back of his head. "You got something else you want changed?" he asked apprehensively.

Miss Buchanan laughed. "No, Joe. I've made my last correction." She turned to the girls. "Joe's the head man here, and I've given him a hard time with my changes on the original plans. But this library has to be built with a look to the future. Bert Long and I agree that it must be as adequate fifty years from now as the day we open."

Em followed the two up the steps. Fifty years from now! she thought. She would be an old, old lady by that time, maybe even a grandmother, but the library would be the same. She might even be dead by then! Stone, tile, and marble had a way of outlasting flesh, bone and muscle. It was a sobering thought.

Across the threshold they entered the lower lobby. To the right and to the left, broad marble steps led to the upper lobby.

Miss Buchanan pointed above. "All across up there, those broad frames will be glass, to keep outside cold from the stack room, while still letting in some light."

The three mounted the steps to the left. On the landing, Miss Buchanan indicated the doorway ahead. "That will be my office, where I'll do the cataloguing. The room beyond will be the Library Board room."

Jessie pointed to the long flight of marble stairs leading to the second floor. "What's upstairs?"

"We can't go up there yet; the floors aren't in. But there is an auditorium that will seat four hundred and fifty people. There are several small rooms for meetings and one very large one in which I hope to start a museum. It's high time we began collecting things relating to the early days of this county. I'm sure lots of people would have interesting items to donate." The librarian stepped across the threshold into the upper lobby. "Now, over there will be the charging desk, with book stacks behind it and on each side. This floor will be tile like in the lower lobby."

"Whew!" Em exclaimed. "It's so big and imposing. Those marble pillars are magnificent."

"I guess we better not go any farther; our skirts will get so dirty. But down there to the right through that arch is the main reading room where we'll have magazines and newspapers, tables and comfortable chairs. There's lots of wall space in that room; I hope in time to have some fine paintings there." The librarian pointed to the left at the opposite end of the upper lobby. "That's to be the children's room. I have ordered low tables and small chairs for it."

Em lifted her skirts above her ankles and walked over to look at the children's room. "Oh, do come and see, Jessie. Look, there's going to be a fireplace. My young brother, Vic, is going to love this place. You have young brothers and sisters too, don't you?"

"Yes, four, two of each. Oh, Em, aren't we lucky to have jobs here? I can scarcely believe it. To think, of all the girls in town, Miss Buchanan chose us!"

Em turned and looked at the slender girl beside her. Jessie's dark eyes were deep-set. Black hair, framing her sensitive face, was coiled in a large knot at the nape of her neck. There was no doubt about it, Em decided, Jessie was a real beauty. It was a wonder she wasn't married. Em was sure that if she were a man, Jessie would be just the kind of girl she would select for a wife. Probably Jessie didn't have time for beaux. Now if Ashton were home and saw Jessie—! Em's fanciful mind quickly slipped off into one of her frequent fantasies.

By the time Ashton finished medical school and got established, Jessie's brothers and sisters would be old enough to go to work and Jessie would be free to marry. What a beautiful bride she would be, walking down the aisle of a church. Maybe Jessie would ask her, Em, to be a bridesmaid.

Em blinked her eyes, realizing that she hadn't heard Jessie's remark. "What did you say?"

Jessie laughed. "You look miles away, Em. I said, we better go. Miss Buchanan went outside. What do you hear from your brother? I heard he had joined the army."

Em smiled, wondering what Jessie would think if she knew the picture she had been imagining. "He's in Florida, getting ready to go to Cuba. We had a letter just yesterday." She must invite Jessie to supper some evening. If she talked to her a lot about Ashton she might arouse her interest. She would write to Ashton and describe Jessie. It would be fun playing cupid for these two.

Outside, Miss Buchanan and Joe were seated on a stone ledge at the side of the steps.

"We are ahead of schedule, Miss Buchanan," the man was saying. "It just might be that we'll get her finished early and you could move in before the first of the year."

"Splendid." The librarian looked up at her two assistants. "Hear that, girls? We've got a lot of planning and hard work ahead of us. Besides getting our book collection moved and in place, we must plan a dedication ceremony that Harper City will never forget."

It was after one o'clock when Em got home. Mama had just hung up the dishpan.

"Well, how is Miss Dudley, the librarian?" she asked.

"Mama, you have no idea how grand the new library is! It's all tile and marble and beautiful woodwork! And the size of it! Why it's almost like a palace. And the man in charge of the workmen says we may be able to move in before the first of the year."

"What a great day for Harper City when it does open,"

Mama said, spreading the dish towel on a rod near the stove. "I suppose Bert Long and the rest of the Library Board will take credit for getting it, but Jenny was the yeast that set the whole idea going."

"Is Papa asleep?"

"No. He didn't get to lie down. One of the Nichols boys came to get him. I suppose it's Mrs. Nichols' time. I wonder if it will be twins again. Papa would like you to go down to his office to hold the fort till he gets there. I don't think he'll be long; Mrs. Nichols usually has an easy time. Come along to the sitting room with me. I want you to take some of the magazines we have finished reading down to the office."

Two women and a man with a bandaged hand were already in the doctor's office by the time Em got there. She told them that her father was out on a call, but that she expected him within an hour or so. One of the ladies decided to do some errands and return later.

Em straightened the magazines on the table in the center of the room and put down those she had brought from home. She turned to the man. "How's your hand coming along, Mr. Blain?"

"Oh, all right, I guess. It doesn't pain me much anymore. Doc says it'll be stiff for a while. Guess I was lucky he was able to save all the fingers. Are those some newer magazines you just put there? I've read all of Doc's old ones."

Em picked up one. "Here's *McClure's* for May."

Mr. Blain took the periodical and leafed through its pages. "Guess it's too soon to have any articles about this Cuban situation. What do you hear from Ashton?"

"The last letter was from Florida." Em turned to the woman. "Mrs. Sawyer, here's the May issue of the *Ladies' Home Journal* if you want it."

The woman raised her eyes from a magazine. "No, thank you Emeline. This old *Munsey's* is all right. It's been such a long time since I have been to see the doctor that even his oldest magazines are new to me."

Em went into her father's examination room and returned with a dust cloth. She dusted the front window sills first, pausing to look out the open windows at the town square below. Buggies, carriages and wagons stood around the Court House, the horses tied to the hitching rail. Benches on the Court House lawn provided resting places for those who had come to town for the day. Children ran about playing tag under the watchful eyes of their parents.

The dusting finished, Em straightened Papa's examination room and washed some instruments. She was just drying her hands, when loud screams seemed to fill the whole building.

Em quickly opened the door to the hall. Up the stairs from a street came a screaming woman leading a boy; the blood from a wound on his forehead flowed down over his white shirt. The boy was pale, but not a sound came from his tightly closed mouth.

Em met them at the top of the stairs, took the boy's arm and guided him into the examination room.

The mother looked about. "Where's Doctor Dudley? Where is he? Where is he?" she screamed.

Em picked up the injured boy and put him on the examination table. "Mrs. Sawyer," she called out through the open door to the waiting room, "will you help me?"

Mrs. Sawyer came in. "What can I do, Emeline?"

"Take care of her, while I see to this." Em wet a towel and put it on the wound. With another she wiped the boy's face. "You are a brave one not to cry. What's your name?"

"Billy Sessions."

Mrs. Sawyer tried to soothe the weeping mother. "Now,

now, dry your eyes. I've had five boys and I can't tell you the number of times they've come home bloodier than this, and all of them are grown men now."

"But he's all I have. Where is Doctor Dudley?"

"He will be here soon, Mrs. Sessions. Why don't you go in the other room. I'll take care of Billy until my father comes."

The mother's sobs lessened. "Oh, are you the doctor's daughter?"

Em nodded. This seemed to reassure the distraught woman and she allowed Mrs. Sawyer to lead her out.

Em shut the door. "Well, Billy, let's see this head of yours," she said, imitating Papa's casual manner in an emergency. She took the towel away revealing a long deep gash across the forehead. Papa would have to take some stitches in this one, she surmised. "Now you lie very still." She washed the wound, then covered it again with a wet towel. "Where do you live, Billy?"

"On Fifth Street. We just moved here last week." The boy watched Em closely as she washed the blood from his hands.

"From where?"

"Chicago."

"So—you're a big city boy." Em took a granite tray and began assembling the instruments Papa would need when he arrived. She continued to talk calmly to the injured boy, grateful that Mrs. Sawyer had succeeded in quieting the noisy mother.

In a few minutes the doctor entered the examination room from the hall. "Well, what have we here, daughter?" he asked, putting down his bag and removing his coat.

"This is Billy Sessions, Papa. He has a little nick on his head that needs your attention. He's new in town. Moved here from Chicago."

"From Chicago, heh?" Dr. Dudley washed his hands, picked up a towel and stood beside the table, smiling down at the boy as he dried his hands. "That's quite a city. That's where I learned to be a doctor."

Em held the boy's hands while her father examined the injury. How gentle Papa was, and yet his touch was strong and sure.

The ordeal over, Billy sat up and looked at himself in the mirror Em held before him. "How do you like it, Billy?" she asked.

"Gee! Wait till the kids on my block see this. I bet none ever had a bandage like it." Billy touched the white wrappings around his head.

The doctor laughed. "That's right. And you tell them that Doc Dudley had to take four stitches to hold you together."

Billy hopped off the table and ran into the waiting room. "Ma! Ma! The doctor put four stitches in me!"

On her way home Em thought what a nice little fellow Billy Sessions was. She supposed it was because of Vic that she felt she understood small boys. If she weren't committed to being a librarian, she might be interested in working as a nurse for children. Often in the last two years she had helped Papa treat them at his office. She could still feel the warm clasp of Billy's hands as Papa had tended his head.

The following Saturday, Virginia Miller gave a picnic supper for the members of H.C.B.C. In the Millers' side yard a long table was well filled with fried chicken, potato salad, baked beans and cole slaw. By the time large wedges of strawberry shortcake were placed before them, the girls ate more slowly and talked.

"I was wondering what you girls would think of our club riding out to Shafers' Mill next Tuesday morning," Virginia said as she passed a large pitcher of cream to Dottie Leghorn. "Since the weather is so hot, we might each take a lunch and go wading in the river in the afternoon."

Em spoke up. "I couldn't go Tuesday. I take my library training on Tuesday and Thursday mornings." She took the cream from Dottie and poured some on her shortcake.

"Oh, Em, you do sound so important," Molly Flannery said with a sigh and a widening of her eyes. "You must be awfully smart for Miss Buchanan to have selected you. What do you have to know to work in a library?"

Enjoying the attention, Em lifted her head with a little toss and smiled. "Just about everything I guess. Or at least you have to know in what book to find what you *don't* know. But of course," she added modestly, "I won't really know how to be a librarian for a long time. I've only had two days of instruction."

"Girls, I've just had a wonderful idea!" Lucile Jackson put down her spoon. "You know Mama is president of the Browning Society. Well, they have been working on a new project called 'Art for the Library.' Miss Buchanan put the bee in Mama's bonnet. The society has joined forces with the Art Club and the two are raising money to buy paintings for the new building. They have been holding baked goods sales, rummage sales, white elephant sales, and the like. Of course it will take them a long time to get enough for even one painting because Miss Buchanan says she'll have only the best. Now why couldn't we do something like that for the new library? Only we could choose to buy something less expensive, so it wouldn't take us so long to get it."

There was a murmur of approval. "How do you propose we earn money?" Virginia asked.

Lucile picked up her spoon and thoughtfully cut into a strawberry, watching the red juice turn the cream in the dish to a delicate pink. "How many of you have strawberry patches in your gardens?" Six of them did. "Well, if each of you could furnish berries, Madge and I would furnish the cream and we could have a strawberry festival!"

"Where would we have it?"

"Who has the biggest yard in the most central location?" Em spoke up. "I guess I do."

"Will your folks let you have it?"

"I think so," Em answered. "By the way, what will we be working for? People like to know what cause they are helping."

"Em, you know more about the library than any of the rest of us," Virginia stated. "You're the only one who has seen the inside of the building. What is needed?"

Em thought for a moment. "Well, the children's room is going to be lovely, so big, lots of windows, a fireplace, and tables and chairs just the right size for children. But you know how little the children's corner down in the Harper building is; I'm afraid the books there won't even half fill the children's shelves in the new library. How about our bicycle club starting a fund to buy children's books?"

They all talked at once.

"Would Miss Buchanan approve?"

"When should we have the festival?"

"My uncle Ed works at the *Evening News*. I'll ask him to put a story in the paper."

"We have lots of Japanese lanterns in the attic. We can string them in your yard, Em, and have the festival run on after dark."

Em got home at a quarter to nine. Mama was on the porch. Vic and four neighborhood children were running about the yard catching lightning bugs. Papa had not returned yet from his office.

Mama readily assented to the use of the Dudley front lawn for the H.C.B.C.'s strawberry festival the following week. Furthermore, she said, she would bake some cakes; people were bound to pay an extra nickel to have a piece of cake with their berries and cream. "You just as well get ten cents from every customer as five," she said emphatically.

Em explained the project to Papa when he returned. He asked what he could do to help.

"When it's time, help me set up the tables, Papa. The sawhorses and planks are in the haymow, aren't they?"

"That's right. And Emmy, you go down to Mort Gould's undertaking establishment on Monday and see if he'll lend you enough folding chairs for the affair. I'm sure he will if you explain your philanthropic purpose."

In bed, Em's mind went on planning. Tomorrow was Sunday; in the afternoon she would call on Miss Buchanan and get her approval to go ahead on the children's book fund; then she would tell Madge Swanson so that her uncle could put the story in the newspaper. My goodness, they had forgotten all about riding out to Shafers' Mill to wade in the river! Such a thing seemed pretty small potatoes compared to this project for the library—a strawberry festival to provide good books for the younger generation of Harper City!

Chapter 6

Strawberries and Books

Miss Buchanan enthusiastically approved of the H.C.B.C.'s project. "I *have* worried somewhat about the children's room," she confessed to Em. "I had quite a hard time getting the Library Board to let me use that room solely for children's books. They wanted to designate a corner in the adult stack room for juvenile books as now in our present location. They said that room should be another adult reading room. Well, anything worth having is worth fighting for; and you know me, I fought hard. But I must say, knowing the small number of books we have suitable for children, and looking at all the shelf space in that room— A strawberry festival, you say? Very commendable, very commendable."

The newspaper story, announcing the "commendable" affair, emphasized not only the festival and its purpose, but also the Harper City Bicycle Club, giving the names of the eight members.

"It just goes to show," Virginia told Em, "if you try to do a good thing without thinking of reward, you get the reward too."

Em looked doubtful. "I'm not so sure. I know plenty of real saints in this town whose lives are full of good works and who never get any recognition by word of mouth, let alone a newspaper story. We were just lucky. After that publicity, we'll have no trouble at all getting new members."

Even at five o'clock in the morning, on June 15, it was warm. Em, kneeling on a board beside the strawberry patch at the back of the lot, cast frequent glances at the sky. If it rained today she would just die! Everything would be ruined, absolutely ruined! She wondered if the other girls were out of bed yet, picking berries. They had promised to bring their donations to the Dudleys' around ten.

Yesterday when Papa returned from afternoon office hours, he, Vic, Mama and Em had taken the sawhorses and table planks from the haymow. Now six long tables were set up in the front yard. Mr. Gould, the undertaker, had promised Em he would bring the folding chairs this morning.

On the pantry shelves were five cakes, frosted in white icing sprinkled with coconut, chocolate icing dotted with walnut kernels, and caramel icing edged with hickory nuts. And even now, energetic Mama was in the kitchen beating batter for more cakes. Em hoped enough people would come tonight to eat all they were preparing.

The ripe berries picked, Em took the dishpanful to the cellar. Later today the club members would gather to stem and wash them.

It was after seven when the Dudleys sat down to breakfast in the dining room. Mama's baking had made the kitchen too hot to eat there.

The doctor was just taking a second fried egg from the platter, when there was a knock at the kitchen door.

"Ah, me!" he exclaimed. "Wonder who has a bellyache this early in the morning. Pass the pepper, please, Nellie. I'm going to finish my breakfast before I go."

"I'll see who it is, Papa." Em rose from the table.

On the back porch stood Jeff Wayne, a bucket of strawberries in his hand.

"Good morning, Em. I read about that club of yours and the strawberry festival you are having tonight. I figured you might need some more berries. So I picked ours this morning. Can you use them?"

Em smiled, hoping he wouldn't notice the dirt on the front of her calico morning dress. She hadn't had time to change since coming in from the garden. "Indeed we can. Come on in. I picked ours this morning too. I expect the other girls to come with theirs later. Bring those down in the cellar where it's cool."

Jeff followed her across the kitchen and down the cellar steps. He set his full bucket on the table beside Em's crimson-filled dishpan. "If I didn't have to go to work, I'd stay and help stem them," he said. "It's so nice and cool down here, I hate to leave. But I'll be over tonight and if I can help, I'd like to."

"Why, thank you, Jeff. Where are you working?"

"At the bank, but just for the summer. I'm entering Purdue in the fall."

"Are you going to be a banker like your father?" Em asked.

"No, not if I can help it. I'm going to study agriculture. I want to be a farmer."

Em raised her eyebrows. Somehow the occupation seemed out of character for the garrulous, joking Jeff. She could imagine him behind a desk at the bank, but behind a plow? Never! "Is your father pleased with your decision?"

"Goodness no! But he says if I'm bound to be a farmer, I have to be a good one, go to college and learn the latest wrinkles in agriculture." Jeff pushed his bucket to the middle of the table and grinned. "I'm sure he thinks I'll change my mind after four years and be ready to go into banking. He's going to be surprised."

Back in the kitchen, they found the doctor. "Oh, so it's

you, Jeff. I thought I was being called out. You certainly don't look sick."

"No sir, Doctor, I'm not. Just brought some strawberries for Em's festival. What do you hear from Ashton these days?" Jeff stood near the back door.

"We think he's leaving Tampa for Cuba sometime this week." The doctor picked up the coffee pot and walked toward the dining room.

"Well, I hope those Rough Riders and the others get over there and give the Spanish what's coming to them!" Jeff said as he stepped onto the back porch. "Em, I heard a lot of the fellows say they were coming early tonight to see if you girls need any help. You know what? You really should have some masculine members in that club of yours. We ride bicycles too, you know."

Em laughed. "I'll bring that idea up at the next meeting."

When she returned to the dining room Papa was mumbling something about young whippersnappers who knew nothing at all about war, absolutely nothing!

Em wished she had thought to tell Jeff that she was going to be a librarian; it had such a grand sound.

The Dudleys' front lawn was gay that evening. The long tables, usually put up only when the Dudley family reunion took place in Harper City, were filled by the town's citizens.

Virginia Miller sat at a small table by the walk and sold tickets, five cents for a pink one for a dish of strawberries and cream, and five cents for a white one for a slice of Mama's cake.

The rest of the club members, wearing their white graduation dresses and frilly aprons, served the refreshments. They accepted willingly the services of the several young men who turned up early.

At a table alongside the house, Mama washed and dried dishes and spoons. Alex Thompson brought berries from the cellar as they were needed, fetched the cakes, and, when it was dusk, got the stepladder from the barn and lighted the candles in the Japanese lanterns. Em supposed that later Mama would be pointing out his dependability again.

With an empty tray in her hands, Em stepped up on the front porch and looked out across the yard. If only Ashton could see this! Strung the length of the lawn, the lanterns were like large colorful butterflies, fluttering above the tables. How Ashton would love seeing the lanterns they had hung on Blitzen's antlers.

And there was Miss Buchanan moving from table to table, talking, Em was sure, about the new building.

The doctor came up the steps. "Well, Emmy, it looks like your festival is a big success. There's never been this many at any church festival, that I can remember."

"That's probably because the library belongs to everyone, so we are getting people from all the churches. Aren't you home early?"

"Not many patients tonight. They must all be here stuffing themselves with strawberries." He set his bag on the porch stand. "I must get down there and buy some tickets from Virginia. Is there any of Nellie's angel food cake left?"

"Maybe." Em watched him walk toward the front of the yard to the ticket seller's table.

By a quarter to ten there was nothing left of the strawberries but juice, and of the cakes only a few crumbs. The girls helped Em clean the kitchen, while the young men, under the doctor's direction, dismantled the tables and carried them to the barn. They stacked the folding chairs on the porch, then took down the lanterns.

In the sitting room Virginia and Miss Buchanan spread the money on the table and began to count, with Mrs.

Dudley looking on. Stacks of pennies, nickles, dimes, quarters, and fifty-cent pieces were arranged in dollar groups for easy counting.

Finished in the kitchen, Em led the others into the room to watch. Mama put her finger to her lips so that they would not disturb the counters.

Miss Buchanan wrote down some figures. "Well, Virginia, I make it forty-two dollars and ninety-five cents. Does that tally with your count?"

"Exactly!" Virginia put down her pencil and looked up at the other club members. "Well, I'd say our first project was a success, girls. What do you think, Miss Buchanan?"

The librarian took off her spectacles and rubbed the imprint on her nose. "Well, I'd say you've done a good deed for the library, right enough. Now, Jessie, Em, and I will have to see that we buy only the best children's books with this money. The best is none too good for Harper City young ones."

"I hate to break up this party," the doctor said at the door, "but it's late. Girls, there are some young fellows on the porch waiting to take you home. And Jenny, I'm going to escort you."

"Nonsense, Maylen, there's no need."

Em followed the others to the porch and watched them pair off and saunter down the walk. Only Alex remained.

"Em, may I call on you tomorrow evening?"

Em swallowed a yawn. She was tired and very sleepy. Having Alex around tomorrow night didn't appeal to her at the moment. Still he had worked hard this evening and was always exactly where he was needed. "Why if you want to, Alex."

"Would half-past seven be too early?"

"I guess not."

"Good night, Em."

"Good night, Alex. And thanks for all your help. We could not have gotten along without you."

She watched him. As he turned toward town she heard him softly whistling "Billy Boy."

In her room, dressed in her nightgown, Em brushed her hair, braided it and blew out the lamp. Kneeling on the floor before the open window, she looked at the stars. Far in the distance the faint rumble of thunder had an ominous sound. It might rain before morning. Thank goodness it had held off this evening. At the edge of town, a train whistle tooted mournfully, followed shortly by the roar of a freight bumping over the Big Four tracks on Third Street.

How was she going to deal with Alex? Did she want to encourage him? He was a nice fellow and, she had to admit, very likable *and* dependable. If Ashton were here he could advise her. She and Ashton used to sing that song together.

> Oh, where have you been Billy Boy, Billy Boy?
> Oh, where have you been, charming Billy?
> I have been to seek a wife,
> She's the joy of my life,
> She's a young thing and cannot leave her mother.

Before getting into bed she prayed a long prayer for Ashton's safety.

Next morning at the library, Miss Buchanan spoke to Em about how they would use the bicycle club's money. "I thought about it last night," the librarian said. "We want to be careful about what we buy for the children's collection. I'd like you and Jessie to help with the selection. If you and she could get together soon, go over the book advertisements in the magazines for the past year or so, and make a list of the new children's books, giving the authors, titles, prices and publishers, then later the three of us could decide which ones we want to buy."

"Do you think Jessie and I know enough to help in such a decision?" Em asked.

"You will learn. I aim to give you girls guided experience." The librarian looked out the window thoughtfully. "You know, when I was at library school several years ago, they recommended a publication called *Books for the Young;* it was a list of the best juvenile books, compiled by a librarian in the East. I must look up my notes and get her name. It might be a valuable investment for us to get a copy."

When Em went home at noon she carried several copies of the *Atlantic Monthly, Harpers* and *McClure's Magazine.* After dinner she sat on the front porch and concentrated on the book advertisements. At one-thirty she decided that she and Jessie should do this together as Miss Buchanan had suggested.

She rode her bicycle across town to the Overstreets' small cottage on Euclid Avenue. Mrs. Overstreet was giving a fitting in the bedroom and Jessie was bent over the sewing machine in the dining room. Em explained her errand, asking when Jessie would be free to work with her.

"I could come this evening by seven," Jessie answered. "I'd ask you to come here but it's pretty noisy, what with the children and the sewing machine."

It wasn't until Em was putting her bicycle in the barn that she remembered. She had told Alex he might come over tonight! Oh, well, he would just have to sit quietly while she and Jessie did this job.

Jessie came at seven, spoke to Mama, seated on the porch, then went inside where she and Em spread the magazines on the sitting room table.

"How do you think we should do this, Jessie?" Em asked, pulling two straight chairs to the table.

"Well, I suppose Miss Buchanan would order them by writing to the publishers, so why don't we list the books under their publishers."

"Good idea." Em opened a magazine. "Not all publishers do children's books. Shall I call out when I find some?"

"Yes, and I'll write it down. Then, later, we can change jobs. What's first?"

"Hmm. Here are two published by Houghton, Mifflin. I guess you better put the address down too." Em stopped while Jessie wrote. "The title of the first is *Three Little Daughters of the Revolution* by Nora Perry. That sounds good. I always loved stories that had some history in them, didn't you?" Jessie nodded. Em went on. "The second is *A Little Girl of Long Ago* by Eliza Orne White. Just a minute, I better give you the prices too. The first one was seventy-five cents and the second one dollar." Em turned a page. "Oh, here's one by Laura Richards, a new edition of *Captain January.*"

"The same publisher?"

"No. It's Dana Estes and Company of Boston. But maybe you better not put down that title, it costs two-fifty. It says here that it is 'The 100th Thousand of this charming little classic.' They probably have a cheaper edition. But, say, Jessie, on second thought, go ahead and write it down. Maybe the illustrations are extra special. Miss Buchanan might want to get it. I'd love to see it myself. Laura Richards was one of my favorite authors."

"Any others under that publisher?"

"Here's one Vic would love—*When Israel Putnam Served the King* by James Otis, a story of the French and Indian war. It costs seventy-five cents."

The room was quiet as Em scanned the pages and Jessie wrote. Em looked up. "Head another page with this publisher, Doubleday and McClure. They are publishing a dog story, *Bob, Son of Battle* by Alfred Ollivant and it costs one dollar and a quarter." She turned the page. "Oh, Jessie, here is an author I must tell you about. His books are listed here. Stephen Crane! My brother Ashton talked to him." Em launched into the story of the young reporter in Tampa.

"Shall I write down his books?"

"Oh, no, they're not for children. Did you ever meet Ashton?" Em asked.

"No."

Em got up and took Ashton's photograph from the mantel. She held it near the lamp. "This was taken about a year ago."

Jessie looked up at the picture. "He's very good-looking."

Em returned the photograph to the mantel and began describing Ashton. Here was a wonderful chance to get this romance started. Tomorrow she would write to Ashton about Jessie. "And he has the most wonderful sense of humor," she went on. "Once when Vic was about seven, Ashton—"

There was a step in the hall. Alex appeared in the doorway. "Excuse me, Em, your mother said I should come on in. Oh, hello, Jessie."

"Alex, you're just in time to help two very new and inexperienced librarians. Pull up a chair." Em smiled up at him.

"Hello, Alex," Jessie said, putting down her pencil. "We could do with a man's point of view. You can help us choose the kinds of books boys like. So far we've had to rely on the tastes of our brothers."

Alex sat at the end of the table. They worked until

nine, when Mama brought in some lemonade and cookies.

At a quarter to ten Em stood on the front porch and watched Jessie and Alex leave together. Of course it had only been natural for Alex to offer to see Jessie home. But what if Alex interfered with her plans for Ashton and Jessie? She frowned and went back in the house. Why, she wondered, had the sight of those two going off together disturbed her? Alex really didn't mean anything to her, did he?

She stacked the magazines on the table. "You're late, Papa," she said as the doctor came into the sitting room, took off his coat, and hung it on a chair back.

"Yes. I had to make a house call at the Schmidts. Their baby is ailing again and it's certainly no wonder. Mrs. Schmidt feeds him everything under the sun." The doctor sat down in a rocking chair and stretched his legs out in front of him. "Mama gone to bed?"

"Yes. See all these lists of children's books Jessie and I made? Alex was here too and helped."

"That boy seems to enjoy helping around here. Is he going to be camping on our front porch the rest of the summer?"

Em frowned and turned away. "I don't think so. At least not after tonight. You see, Jessie hasn't been in school this past year and during that time she has grown into just about the most beautiful girl in town. It could be that from now on, Alex will be sitting on the Overstreets' front porch. At least he seemed awfully glad to take her home tonight."

"So? Does that bother you?"

Em hesitated. "Not really, I guess. But you see, Papa, I had another romance in mind for Jessie."

"Anyone I know?"

Em nodded. "Now, don't laugh, Papa, but I thought she and Ashton would be a wonderful couple."

The doctor smiled, crossed his legs and ran his fingers through his graying hair. "Emmy Lou, let me give you a little advice; don't ever try to be a matchmaker. You'll come out at the little end of the horn every time. There's no accounting for tastes when it comes to looking for a life partner. How would you like someone to choose a husband for you?"

"Oh, I'm not going to get married. I'm just going on working with Miss Buchanan for years and years." Em tried to speak lightly.

"What! And give me no grandchildren! You'll change your tune one of these days."

"Well, maybe so. But in the meantime I'm going to be the best librarian I can. Maybe some summer I can go to Chicago and take that same library course Miss Buchanan took. Good night, Papa."

"Good night, Emmy Lou." The doctor gave her a hug.

Em went upstairs. Why, she wondered, did she still have this twinge at the thought of Alex walking beside Jessie? Hadn't she been trying to think of ways to discourage his attention to herself? What was she? A dog in the manger?

Chapter 7

Americans All

As June wore on, Em and Jessie continued their twice-a-week library instruction periods with the intrepid Miss Buchanan. From the lists of children's books the two girls had prepared, the librarian had samples of their handwriting. Jessie, she said, had a good round library hand, but Em's would not do; it was not legible enough. Therefore, Em must learn to use the typewriter in the back room.

The morning sun beat in the east library windows, making the back room extremely hot. Em grew to dislike the time spent there at the typewriter, pounding out page after page of the learning exercises. F-G-H-J-, space, F-G-H-J-, space! The letters grew positively nauseating! How long would Miss Buchanan keep her on this lesson? She knew the answer to that. Until she could produce five faultless pages of the boring exercise without looking at the keys.

Afternoons, at home, Em stretched out in the hammock strung between the cherry tree and the grape arbor in the back yard and read. She had asked Miss Buchanan what books a librarian should be reading. Now she perused the suggested volumes: new ones, old ones, exciting ones, dull ones, romantic and humorous; she poured them into her mind with determined fervor. The budding librarian, formerly an avid reader of the light Prisoner-of-Zenda variety of fiction, now delved into *Middlemarch*, *Les Miserables*, and *Anna Karenina*. She *would* be well-read, she vowed, or know the reason why! There was so much to catch up on, books written long before she was born. She doubted if she ever would get to the present-day writers Miss Buchanan had suggested.

Late one afternoon Papa found her asleep in the hammock, a volume of Carlyle's *French Revolution* opened and lying on her chest. He picked up the book and looked at the title as Em wakened.

"Tarnation, Em! What a thing to be reading on a summer afternoon. Guess Carlyle put you to sleep. How long have you been out here?"

"Since one."

"Humph!" the doctor grunted. "It's not good for you to lie around like this every afternoon. As the doctor looking after your health, I prescribe at least one bicycle ride every day, or a walk."

"But Papa, I'm trying to read all the books on the list Miss Buchanan gave me."

"Well, you don't have to read all the heavy stuff in the library this summer. You are getting circles under your eyes. First thing you know you'll have to have spectacles."

Em sat up, put her feet on the ground and moved the hammock back and forth slowly. "Do you think I would look more like a librarian if I had nose glasses like Miss Buchanan's?"

Papa laughed. "Well, Jenny didn't wear them when she was your age. And you're not going to either, if I can help it." He took her hand, pulled her to her feet and gave her a spank on the seat of her skirt. "Get into the house there and help Mama with supper. Speed up your circulation and get some roses in your cheeks." He followed her to the back door. "Has the *News* come?"

"It isn't time for it yet."

"Judge Hargrove was in late this afternoon to show me Charlie's picture on the front page. Honest-to-goodness, you'd think he was the only man in the country with a boy in the war," Papa grumbled.

Em clasped her book tighter. Charlie's picture in the paper! She wished the newsboy would hurry up with it.

After the supper dishes were done, Em sat on the porch steps and looked at Charlie Hargrove's photograph on the front page of the *News*. He was very handsome and cocky in his Rough Riders uniform; one side of his hat was turned up at a jaunty angle, and there was a self-assured smile on his lips as though, singlehanded, he was about to chase all of the Spaniards out of Cuba.

Em gave a small sigh. She hadn't remembered that he was so good-looking. Perhaps it was the uniform. She recalled that Ashton had written of Colonel Roosevelt's hat being turned up on one side like this. Was Charlie imitating his leader? Well, anyway it was a very becoming way for a fellow to wear a hat; it gave Charlie such an air. She wondered if he would do much reading after the war, if he would ever come in the library. She folded the paper and put it on the step.

Looking dreamily across the yard to the street, she imagined herself behind the charging desk in the new library, and, looking up suddenly at the returned soldier, saying, "Yes, I'm a librarian, now, Charlie. May I help you find a book?" And then she would suggest some of these classics she had been reading so that he would know she was no longer a frivolous high school girl, but a woman who knew literature. Would he want to be a lawyer like his father? If so, he would have to go on to college. She hoped he would stay in Harper City long enough after the war to renew their acquaintance.

Before going to bed, Em got the scissors from her sewing box and cut the picture from the paper. She stuck it in at the frame on her dresser mirror, just above a piece of paper upon which she had typed the list of numbers for the Dewey Decimal System of book classification and the subjects for which they stood.

Every night she repeated the classification to herself. Tonight, however, by the time she got to "700—Fine Arts," her eyes wandered above to Charlie. One gauntlet-gloved hand on hip, he seemed to be saying, "Hello there, Em Dudley."

"Hello, yourself, Charlie Hargrove," she whispered back.

On July 2 the evening newspaper's headlines read:

SAN JUAN HILL TAKEN BY U.S. TROOPS
ROUGH RIDERS TAKE PART IN BATTLE

Em sat quietly on the porch that evening thinking of Ashton and Charlie, praying for their safety. Papa and Mama had eaten very little at supper and Papa had gone to his office without a word of good-bye.

It had been nearly a month since they had heard from Ashton in Tampa. Was he ill? Had he survived this battle? Was Charlie still a whole man or had he been wounded in the Rough Riders' charge? Was that jaunty hat of his trampled in the dirt and blood of the battlefield? The newspaper had said that casualties were relatively light, but if one of those casualties was your brother or fellow classmate, then the loss was heavy indeed. Those few casualties had to belong to someone.

On the Fourth of July the resounding boom of a cannon cracker on the next street wakened Em at six. Later in the morning, with other members of the bicycle club, she listened to speeches delivered from the bunting-draped platform on the Court House lawn. Thoughts of the "relatively light casualties" kept her from giving full attention to the oratory.

On Wednesday morning, July 13, she sat on the porch to watch for the mailman. There probably would be nothing. Except on the mornings she was at the library, she had kept this vigil every day since July 1.

Spotting the mail carrier two blocks away, she walked down to the gate to wait. He saw her as he came off the Randalls' porch. He waved, then reached into his leather bag and pulled out a letter.

"Good luck this morning, Emmy Lou. Here it is, that letter from Ashton at last!"

"Oh, thank you, Mr. Wallace." She hurried down the sidewalk to meet him and took the letter. "We've been so worried ever since that battle."

The mailman shifted his bag, took a handkerchief from his pocket and wiped his face. "I know. Mrs. Hargrove and the judge are always watching for me too. It's mighty hard sometimes being a postman. A body has to disappoint so many folks. But it's good to see faces light up when the expected letter does come at last. Glad I could put a smile on your face this morning."

Em ran up the steps and into the house, calling out, "Mama, we got a letter from Ashton!"

Mrs. Dudley took the letter, scanned the address in the familiar handwriting, and touched the stamp as though she were caressing the face of the writer.

"Thank God," she said softly. "He must have survived that battle; the postmark is July 5. Put it on the dining room table, Em. It's a fat one. Ashton always was thoughtful, writing us in detail of whatever he was doing. Everything children do is of interest to their parents, even the most humdrum sort of thing, but few children seem to realize that."

"It's a good thing I'm not the one away from home." Em laughed as she took the letter. "I hate to write letters."

As soon as the doctor drove around the house, Vic ran to the barn to tell him about the letter.

"Suppose you wait to lift dinner, Nellie," the doctor said as he passed through the kitchen. "Let's read our letter before we eat."

The others sat at their places around the table as the doctor put on his glasses, opened the letter and read:

Dear Family,

It is 5 A.M. and since I cannot sleep I shall try to give you a picture of this war as I have lived it in the last few days. It seems a lifetime since I last wrote to you from Tampa. I imagine I could write a book about those horrible days at sea on the transport. We boarded June 14 and landed on June 22. It was, I think, the largest military expedition ever to leave the United States. I heard there were 15,058 enlisted men and 819 officers, added to these, of course, were army wagons, horses and mules, cannons, guns and only seven ambulances. The last item, from a doctor's point of view, seemed entirely inadequate.

Jammed together on the crowded troopships, we sweltered under the hot sun. Many became ill with fever; fortunately only malaria showed up, and not typhoid as I constantly feared. Those not suffering from fever were often seasick, I among them. We all lost weight on that voyage. I would have had trouble eating even Mama's cooking, but the hardtack, cold, canned, gray-colored beef, and canned beans I found impossible to swallow.

At daybreak on June 20 we sighted the rugged mountains of the Sierra Maestra, but we did not land at Daiquiri until June 22 after our guns had bombarded the shore.

Our landing was as haphazard as the rest of the operations. Small landing boats rammed into one another, capsizing some.

I saw two Negro soldiers slip as they climbed from a small boat to the pier. They were crushed by an oncoming boat before they could be rescued. They were from the Tenth Cavalry that is made up entirely of Negroes and commanded by First Lieutenant John J. Pershing, who, because of his unit, has been nicknamed Black Jack.

Several boats capsized in the heavy sea. Horses were unloaded by throwing them overboard, leaving them to swim ashore. Remarkably only five or six drowned. I saw a group of cavalry horses start to swim out to sea. An alert bugler on shore saw them too. He put his bugle to his lips and blew the proper call. It was exciting to see those animals wheel around and head for shore.

Things were uncomfortable on shore, but I was so glad to have solid ground under my feet I didn't even mind the mosquitoes too much; and what swarms and swarms of them there are in this place.

Our troops cheered the first Cuban soldiers we saw. We yelled, *"Viva Cuba libre"* and they yelled back, *"Vivan los Americanos."* We forgot the discomfort of the last few days and were fired with the thought of freeing these people.

Our men readily shared their rations with Cuban soldiers and refugees. But, even before we met the Spanish, many of our troops became disgusted with the Cubans. They seemed to regard every American as a charitable institution and expected him to give shirt, coat, or trousers along with his food ration. Personally I feel these Cubans cannot be expected to act otherwise, they have been treated so badly, even savagely by the Spaniards for so long.

None of us slept much that first night; troopships were being unloaded until two in the morning. Men bathed in the surf, trying to wash away the filth of the "prison transports" as they called them. Some ran out of the water to dance naked around the camp fires, shrieking and laughing. It was weird and I felt unreal and in another world, and then—I found Charlie Hargrove!

Papa stopped reading, lifted his eyes to the family. "Well, can you beat that! Meeting Charlie Hargrove in that God-forsaken place!"

Em took her elbows off the table and clenched her hands in her lap. "Go on and read, Papa. Go on."

The doctor continued.

From that moment reality returned. Sitting on a rock some distance from the light of the fires, we talked about home. Home takes on all sorts of virtues and beauty when a fellow is in a strange and forbidding land; things you take for granted when you're there; things like soap and water, three good meals a day, a clean bed at night and a family to love and to love you. I tell you Charlie and I talked for hours about Harper City.

Charlie has grown up fast; he cuts quite a figure in his Rough Riders uniform. His admiration for Colonel Roosevelt is akin to hero worship, but that's healthy at his age. A boy needs a man to follow and look up to. Colonel Roosevelt is all right even though at times a little too cocky for my taste.

I took part in the assault on San Juan Hill on July 1. I don't know what you have read, but the battle almost fought itself. General Shafter was sick, his great hulk exhausted by heat, and, I suspect from what I hear, a realization that he was entirely inadequate to direct the battle.

The fact that the Spaniards had smokeless powder and we did not was a great handicap. No sooner had our guns opened fire than great clouds of white smoke hung over our position giving the Spaniards our location. Shrapnel from their batteries rained on us like hail in a midsummer storm. Men dropped all around me, some killed outright, others wounded and writhing in agony. I longed to drop my gun and go to them, but doctoring and healing were not my job at the moment.

I shall only be able to go on living with myself by forgetting that battle, if I can. By some miracle I was not hit. At one point a thought flashed in my mind—what was happening to Charlie? The Rough Riders were attacking Kettle Hill on our flank. By now I suppose you have read of the bravery of Colonel Roosevelt as he led his men up the hill. I hope the newspaper accounts have told that the Negro regulars of the ninth were intermingled with the Rough Riders in that charge and gave a magnificent account of themselves.

Once when the Spanish fire was very heavy we were ordered to lie flat in the tall grass. A short way in front of me a man arose and peered up at the enemy through field glasses. He was not a soldier but a war correspondent, conspicuously dressed in a white raincoat. It was that fellow I told you about before, the author, Stephen Crane. An officer near me ordered him to lie down. Crane pretended not to hear and moved farther up the hill surveying the scene as though he were watching a Sunday School picnic. The officer called him again, saying if he didn't lie down he would be killed. Crane again ignored the officer. It was then that I spoke up, scarcely realizing that I did so. "What the devil do you think you're doing?" I yelled. "Trying to impress us with your bravery? We don't need any show-offs here."

That got him. He dropped to his knees as I hoped he would. The rest of us breathed easier for the moment.

Well, as you know, we held the hill, but by a very meager margin. At the time we did not realize the importance of our victory. Next morning, because an officer had heard of my knowledge of medicine, I was assigned to a medical group that was to give first aid to the wounded on the battlefield and carry them back to the hospital. It was a harrowing experience. The heat, the blazing sun and the mosquitoes, made the place a living hell for those still breathing. Again and again as I put water to parched lips and bound up gaping wounds, I thought: the dead are the lucky ones. My fear about too few ambulances was borne out. We could have used four times as many.

About midmorning I found Charlie Hargrove, his elbow shattered, a long gash across his forehead where, luckily, a bullet had only grazed the flesh. He was unconscious, otherwise he would have been in agony with that elbow.

Papa, I think you should tell the Hargroves that he is getting along well now. I don't know what kind of word the War Department has sent them. I stayed with him long enough to talk the surgeon out of amputating his arm. Here, where there are few doctors and facilities, amputations are numerous, a quick way to avoid gangrene, I suppose. But I was bound Charlie shouldn't lose his arm. I'm afraid I made myself very unpopular with a certain army surgeon.

This letter is turning out to be a book, but I'll have to stop—paper's about used up. Getting some of my thoughts expressed makes me feel better. The sun is up now and hotter than yesterday.

Looking back on my experiences of the last few days, one thing stands out, the unity of the men here—white regiments, black regiments, regulars, Rough Riders, some from the North some from the South, some contingents commanded by ex-Confederate officers. Regional and racial differences have been forgotten. We are Americans all, facing Spanish bullets together.

Save this letter. Who knows, I might really want to write a book some day.

Love to all,
Ashton

Those around the table were silent as the doctor folded the sheets of the letter and stuffed them back in the envelope.

Em's eyes were moist as she thought of Charlie wounded in that far-off place. Thank God, Ashton had been able to save his arm. Dear Ashton, surely he was spared in that battle for a special reason.

"Maylen," Mama said, "don't you think we should have a prayer of thankfulness? Surely God was looking out for our boy."

"Yes, Nellie." The doctor and his family bowed their heads while he said a simple prayer of gratitude to the Almighty. Mama and Em went to the kitchen to get the food. The doctor stepped into the hall, wound the crank at the side of the telephone on the wall, and gave central the Hargroves' number.

As Em set down the steaming platter of roast pork she heard Papa say, "Hello, Judge, this is Doc Dudley. Just had a letter from Ashton." Then he was silent, listening to the verbose judge. At length, he tried to break in, "But Judge, that's what I want to tell you. Ashton was the one who found him."

As the doctor sat down at the head of the table he grumbled, "Someday I'm going to muzzle the judge and talk for hours about Ashton. According to him it was Charlie who led Colonel Roosevelt and the Rough Riders up that hill to victory."

"What did he say about Ashton saving Charlie's arm?" Em asked.

"The old windbag never gave me a chance to tell him!"

"Oh, well, that's all right," Mama soothed. "Ashton wouldn't want you to brag about him."

Em had small appetite. Now that he was wounded, would Charlie come home? she wondered.

Chapter 8

Letter from New York

When surrender came in Cuba on July 17, the *News* brought out an "Extra" describing the ceremony that took place in the city of Santiago.

General Shafter, other generals and their staffs, met General Toral and one hundred Spanish soldiers. The Spanish troops presented arms, and the Spanish flag, which for three hundred and eighty-two years had floated over the city, was pulled down and furled forever. . . . At noon, before thousands of spectators in the municipal plaza, the officers lined up to witness the raising of the American flag over the Governor's Palace.

A few days later, at a meeting of the bicycle club, the girls chattered at length about the war and the surrender. Em had brought Ashton's letter and read it aloud. The girls were properly impressed and Em basked in the glow of their admiration of her brother.

"How old is Ashton?" Molly Flannery asked.

"He'll be twenty-five in October."

"Oh, shoot! I wish he weren't so old. Well, anyway, Charlie Hargrove is our age. Didn't he look handsome in that newspaper picture? You want to know something? I cut that picture out and put it in my diary."

Em frowned with annoyance. What right did Molly

have to—? Then she laughed silently at herself. How foolish she was to think of Charlie as her own special romantic interest. Probably every girl in town had cut that picture from the paper and dreamed of meeting him when he
returned.

Next day she took Ashton's letter to the library for
Miss Buchanan to read. When the librarian finished, she
looked up and Em thought she saw tears in her eyes.

"That Ashton!" Miss Buchanan exclaimed. "Even as a
small boy he was always quite serious and thoughtful of
others. I remember when he brought you in here for the
first time; you must have been about three. I can just
see him lifting you up on a small chair and showing you
a picture book."

Em nodded. "He read to me a lot."

"When he starts practicing medicine he'll be a great
doctor. I may even give in to a few ailments myself just
to see him in action." The librarian smiled and handed
the letter back to Em.

"You and I will be so busy in the new library by then,
Miss Buchanan, that we'll have no time for sickness," Em
said, putting the letter in her pocketbook.

"Speaking of the new library, Em, reminds me. I think
you have progressed enough in your typing to copy some
letters for me. I have had inquiries from other cities in
Indiana wanting to know how we went about getting a
Carnegie library." Miss Buchanan took a large brown
envelope from the work table drawer. "In here is a copy
of the first letter the Library Board wrote to Mr. Carnegie,
also the reply sent to us by his secretary. Be very careful of them, for I intend to preserve them as historical
documents. In years to come someone may be interested
in learning how we got our fine library building. I want
you to make six first copies of each letter. Carbons won't

do for this purpose. There are four inquiries already; I'd like two in reserve. Also I want copies of this sheet, showing exact costs. Since we are lucky enough to be getting a new library, I'd like to help other cities get them too."

It was raining outside and the back room was cool. Em got the paper and sat down at the typewriter, pleased to be working on something other than the monotonous practice exercises. She rolled in a sheet of paper, propped the letter up with some books, poised her fingers on the proper keys and began.

March 1, 1897

Mr. Andrew Carnegie
New York City, N.Y.

Dear Sir:

Knowing of your generous and substantial interest in aiding the establishments of Public Libraries, we beg to submit the following facts concerning conditions in Harper City, Indiana, in the hope that they may appeal to your interest and pave the way for a fuller presentation of this matter to you.

Harper City is located in the central part of Indiana, sixty-three miles from Indianapolis. It is one of the cities in which the discovery of natural gas has caused the population to increase rapidly. In the last fifteen years our population has grown from 4,000 to more than 17,000 at the present time.

Em looked up from the letter and at the paper in the typewriter. Only two mistakes! Not bad! She erased, typed in the corrections, then continued.

During this period of rapid growth the school population has grown from 800 children to 5,468; the number of school buildings from 3 to 14 and the number of teachers from 12 to 86.

Em took her hands from the keys. Good gracious! She had no idea Harper City had grown that fast in fifteen years. She had been so busy growing herself that she had just taken her hometown for granted. A librarian, she supposed, should pay attention to civic matters like these. She went on typing.

Now we feel the need to enlarge another phase of our educational facilities, namely our library. From the first establishment of our library in 1880 our book collection has grown from 1,400 books to 8,600 books at the present. At the beginning the library was open one day a week. Now we employ a full-time librarian and the library is open every weekday from 9 to 6 and two evenings until 9 P.M.

Some recent legislation gives us a 10-cent levy which amounts to between seven and eight thousand dollars annually.

The library has never had a permanent home since its organization. Our present location is entirely inadequate to hold our book collection and we are compelled to seek larger quarters. With this end in view we have purchased a lot centrally located, but as yet are unable to see how we can secure money to build a suitable building, one that will be adequate for future needs.

We submit these facts to you in the hope that they may appeal to your generosity. Should you be sufficiently interested to desire further information we will gladly submit same, either through correspondence or personal interview.

> *Respectfully submitted,*
> Albert C. Long, President
> Forest L. Gilbert, Secretary
> Edwin M. Tiller, Treasurer
>
> Library Trustees.

Em took out the paper and reread the entire letter. So, she thought, this was the beginning! And now the beautiful library building on Main Street was almost finished. She picked up the reply, written on Mr. Carnegie's stationery, and propped it in place.

March 19, 1897

Mr. Albert C. Long
Harper City, Indiana

Dear Sir:

If your city will provide a suitable site and pledge itself by resolution of your City Council to spend from taxation not less than $5,000 a year on support of its library, Mr. Carnegie will be glad to give $50,000 for the erection of a suitable building.

> *Respectfully yours,*
> James Bertram
> Secretary to Mr. Carnegie

Em read it again. Well, that was short and to the point. Imagine being so rich that you could hand out $50,000 just like that! She had typed the letter without one mistake. She gave a little squeal of satisfaction as she took it from the typewriter. Oh, she *was* getting good! Those dull old exercises were paying off!

On the sheet with all the costs, she had to look at the keys, since she had not yet learned the fingering for numbers.

Purchase price of lot	$ 6,600.00
Contract price of building	48,424.27
Architect's fee	2,421.21
(5% of contract price)	
Cost of furniture	5,000.00
Total	$62,445.48

Em typed the rest of the morning but by noon had not finished the required number of copies.

"I'm awfully slow, Miss Buchanan. But if I go any faster I make mistakes. I'll come back this afternoon and finish if you want me to."

"That won't be necessary. I'll send sets of these along to Kokomo and Muncie this afternoon. You can finish the rest on Thursday."

At the dinner table Em told the family of her morning's work. Having copied the material so many times, she recited parts of the letters verbatim.

"And that's the way we got our library," she wound up. "Isn't Andrew Carnegie the most generous man you ever heard of?"

Dr. Dudley put down his fork and took a sip of coffee. "Well, I suppose he is, although I expect fifty thousand dollars is to him about like twenty-five is to me. He's a self-made man, that's for sure. He came to this country from Scotland at the age of thirteen. Only in America could such a penniless boy acquire wealth. I read that his first job was in a cotton mill, working from six in the morning until six at night, and his pay was one dollar and twenty cents a week." The doctor cut a piece of meat, speared it with his fork and held it in midair. "When I think of Carnegie I try to concentrate on his philanthropy, his libraries and such; but in spite of all that, I keep remembering an article I read about him written by Hamlin Garland. Garland visited the steel towns where Carnegie made his millions, and contrasted the lavishness of the plants with the pigsty homes of the workers. The conditions were horrible. And then there was the Homestead strike in '92 when Carnegie hired Pinkerton detectives to fight his workers. In the face of all that, his grandstand play of great benevolence seems kind of shabby to me. One wonders if the one can erase the other."

"Maylen, you shouldn't destroy Em's enthusiasm for Mr. Carnegie's gift," Mama admonished. "Surely, even if his money was made by questionable means, it is good that some of it is being spent for so worthy a cause as a library."

"Oh, sure. Don't mind me, Emmy. I'm just a crabby old man, always finding fault." The doctor peppered his potato.

Em got up and brought the coffee pot from the kitchen and filled his cup. "Now that the siege of Santiago is over, Papa, and the Spanish have surrendered, don't you suppose Ashton will be home soon?" she asked. And Charlie too, she silently added.

"Well, it's my hope that he'll return in time to go back to school in September. But we mustn't count on it. The way the War Department has handled this war they'll probably be as slow as molasses about getting our boys out of that fever-ridden place." The doctor shut his mouth firmly as though he had said too much.

"Is the fever worse down there, Maylen? What have you heard?" Mama asked, a slight tremor in her voice.

"Now there's no need for you to worry, Nellie. I just spoke in general terms. Ashton has survived this long. He's a strong, young fellow and knows how to take care of himself. He'll be home shortly, I'm sure." He laid his knife and fork across his empty plate, put a last bite of bread in his mouth and pushed away from the table. "I think I'll forego the pie today. I'm going to drive out to the Gately farm before afternoon office hours. I'm a little concerned about Ed's leg. He cut it with his ax, and it just doesn't seem to be healing right. If only I could make him stay off of it; but it's hard for a man to do that when he's got a big farm."

"Oh, Maylen, you'll miss your nap," Mama said with concern.

"It can't be helped, my dear. I can't risk gangrene in Ed's leg."

"Papa, may I ride out with you?" Em asked impulsively.

"Sure. Glad to have the company of a pretty, young librarian."

Em helped her father harness and hitch Prince to the one-seated buggy and the two of them drove through town and out Somerset Pike.

Wheat fields along the way rippled in the wind like waves on a tawny sea; the green leaves on the tall corn rustled restlessly as though the stalks were stretching their utmost to grow even taller before harvest. The leather fastenings on the shafts creaked rhythmically as Prince's legs moved at a trot down the dusty road.

Em looked out across the fields and up at a barn on the hill. "Pretty isn't it, Papa? The Trottmans' barn makes such a vivid splash of red up there against the blue sky."

"It is indeed! Sometimes I wish I had been a farmer, especially when the land looks as fine as it does today. But farmers have to work too hard. Don't think I'd be up to it."

"Oh, Papa! I'm sure no farmer around here works one bit harder than you do. At least when a farmer goes to bed at night, he can sleep until morning." Em patted his arm affectionately.

"Not if he has a sick animal or when the ewes drop their lambs. A farmer has to be a kind of doctor to all of his livestock."

"Papa," Em began slowly, "I had a feeling that you were hiding something from Mama at dinner. Were you?"

The doctor looked at her a moment, then turned his eyes back to the road stretching in front of Prince. "Well, I didn't see any need of sharing *my* worries with her. I hadn't meant to mention fever as I did. I hope she's forgotten it. Last night I stayed up late to read my new issue of the *Journal of the American Medical Association*. There

was an article in it by Doctor Nicholas Senn, chief surgeon
of the United States Volunteers. He told in detail the
physical condition of our men in Cuba. Disease is causing
almost as many deaths among them as the Spanish bullets.
Bad food, lack of sanitation and continuous rain, are bringing typhoid, amebic dysentery, diarrhea, and malaria. And
to make matters even worse, yellow fever has broken out."

"Yellow fever? Is that worse than malaria?"

"Yes. We don't know much about it. Quinine, however,
is quite effective on malaria. If they don't get those soldiers
out of that unhealthy place soon, God knows what kind
of an epidemic may break out." He let the reins lay loose
in his hands. "You know, Em, what I'm going to do tonight? I'm going to write a letter to Secretary of War
Alger!"

Dr. Dudley's letter to Secretary Alger may or may not
have had any effect on the secretary's plans, but August
newspapers told of Camp Wikoff being prepared at Montauk Point on the tip of Long Island to which transports
began bringing troops from Cuba.

On August 12 papers were signed, and President Mc-
Kinley proclaimed an armistice. With the battles in Cuba
over, the newspapers turned to Camp Wikoff for fresh excitement. Em read with increasing dismay the accounts of
the returning army. In Camp Wikoff, one article said, the
sick and dying were neglected and often mistreated. Irate
letters were published, written by citizens who had gone
there to bring their sons home. The accounts of the ema-
ciated, ill-fed and often thirsty soldiers brought anxiety to
every family whose sons were still in Cuba.

Then, to confuse the issue, an article in another paper
said the soldiers were far from neglected, but in fact were
well cared for. What could they believe? Em wondered.

These days the Dudleys did not look into one another's eyes, fearing that the dread in their minds might show. They had not heard from Ashton since the letter written way back in July. Even Vic was subdued; he closed doors softly and remembered not to shout in the house.

Miss Buchanan stopped asking Em for news of her brother. At H.C.B.C. meetings the girls avoided talking about the war. Em almost wished they hadn't been so thoughtful. The very avoidance of the subject seemed to stab her more sharply than if it were discussed.

On Wednesday morning, September 14, Em stood on the front steps and took a letter from Mr. Wallace. It was addressed to the doctor.

"It's not from Ashton," the mail carrier said. "It's from New York. It might be some news of him," he said hopefully.

Em held the letter, turned it over and over, as though she hoped to see through the envelope. "It may be something about Ashton," she said. "If, if it were—" she could not say it. "Well, if it were the worst, it would come from Washington, wouldn't it, Mr. Wallace?"

"I 'spect so, Emmy. I hope it says he's all right and on his way home. Be sure to tell me tomorrow. I always liked your brother Ashton, such a polite boy, and smart as they come, too."

The rest of the morning Mama and Em eyed the letter on the table every time they passed through the dining room, eyed it with dread, with hope, and then dread again.

Em was at the barn when Papa drove in. As she helped him unharness, she told him about the letter waiting at his place.

The doctor hurried inside, sat at the dining room table,

and, without a glance at the rest of the family, slit the envelope addressed in a strange handwriting. He unfolded the letter and glanced at the signature. "It's from a doctor," he told the others. He read aloud.

Dear Dr. Dudley,

I am writing at the request of your son Ashton, who arrived at Camp Wikoff the first of September. He wants me to reassure you that he is all right, says he hasn't been able to write you since he was stricken with yellow fever two months ago. I suspect that only his own knowledge of medicine has kept him from succumbing to the disease entirely. He is convalescing now but is in a very weakened condition.

He has been mustered out and could go home, but it is my opinion that he should not attempt to make the train trip alone. If, however, you could come and accompany him, I think he would have a better chance of recovery in his home, especially with you there to care for him.

I know if I had a son like him I would want to be supervising his case. What a fine doctor he will be someday. I hope it will be possible for you to come and see after him. It is a miracle that he has survived.

> *Very sincerely,*
> Walter Dennis, M.D.

"Oh, Maylen!" Mama cried out. "Yellow fever!"

"Now, Nellie, didn't this Doctor Dennis say he was recovering?" The doctor rose and walked toward the telephone in the hall. "I'll call Doc Freetag and see if he'll take care of my patients for a few days. I'll leave on the eight thirty-two tonight. Emmy, you pack my shaving things, a few shirts and some collars. I'll take my medical bag, too." He gave central Dr. Freetag's number.

Em rose from the table, dazed at the sudden course of events. Ashton must be terribly sick not to have written;

he was always so considerate, especially about not causing Mama any worry.

"Say, Mama, aren't we going to have dinner?" Vic asked.

"Very sensible of you to remind us, Victor," Mrs. Dudley replied. "We must keep up our strength so we'll be able to care properly for Ashton when he gets here. Em, you don't have to pack Papa's bag this minute. Suppose you beat the mashed potatoes a bit more while I pour the gravy."

That evening Em and Vic walked with their father to the railroad station.

"Is there anything special we should do at home, Papa, to get ready for Ashton?" Em asked.

"Oh, I doubt it. Your mother has kept his room ready all along. Of course, he may not have to stay in bed, but it might be well for him to stay there for a few days to rest up from the trip home. Oh, but it will be good to have that boy home again where I can take care of him."

The eight thirty-two was late, and it was nine o'clock when Em and Vic started home. The poplar trees near the railroad station had shed their leaves. Kicking through them reminded Em that fall was nearly here. Soon the other trees would be blazing with the colors she loved, and in October she would be eighteen.

"We should get a move on, Vic. It's past your bedtime." Em walked a little faster. "Tomorrow is a schoolday."

"Oh, who cares. Besides, Papa said I could come to the station with him. Let's walk through downtown and see the lights." Vic stuck his hands in his pockets.

"Well, all right. But we must walk fast." Em liked to see the downtown square at night too. Street lights gave it such a big-city air.

They paused at Iseley's Big Store to look in the windows, then walked on, passing the darkened library.

At the corner, Vic stopped. "Hey, Sis, isn't that Alex Thompson across the street? Who's the girl with him?"

Em looked. It *was* Alex—and Jessie! Em gave a short laugh. "Yes, it is Alex. The girl is Jessie Overstreet. You remember, she was at our house when we worked on a booklist."

"Oh, sure. She's waving at us."

Em waved back. A feeling of annoyance swept over her. How often had Alex called on Jessie? she wondered. He had not been near the Dudley home since that night he had taken Jessie home. All that interest he had shown in Em, herself, on graduation night, had vanished the minute he had looked at Jessie. Em bit her lip.

The couple waited for them on the corner. "Hello, Em, Vic," Jessie greeted them. "What are you doing downtown this time of night?"

Alex smiled at Em. "We're on our way to the ice cream parlor. Won't you join us?"

Vic's face brightened. "Why, sure—" Feeling Em squeeze his hand tightly, he stopped. Past experience told him that this was a signal for silence.

"Oh no, thank you, Alex. We must get home; it's way past Vic's bedtime. We took Papa to catch the train to New York. He's gone to bring Ashton home from Camp Wikoff."

"Bring him home? Oh, Em, was he wounded?" Jessie asked with concern.

"No. He's had yellow fever."

"Em, could you let me know when he is to get in?" Alex asked. "I think the town band should be at the station to welcome him. From what Jessie told me about his bringing Charlie Hargrove in from the battlefield, he is a real hero. He should have a hero's welcome. I just joined the band, you know; I play the cornet. It was Jessie who suggested I join."

"Why, that's fine, Alex. But I'm not sure it would be appropriate to have the band meet Ashton. After all, he wasn't wounded in battle."

"From what I hear of yellow fever, it's twice as bad as gunshot wounds."

"How did you hear about Ashton helping Charlie, Jessie?" Em asked.

"Miss Buchanan told me. Em, I can hardly wait for the new library to open. How about you?"

Em nodded. "How are your training sessions going?"

"All right, I guess. I hope when we get in the new building I can learn to use the typewriter too. Miss Buchanan said you were doing so well on it." Jessie turned to Vic. "What grade are you in this year, Vic?"

"The sixth." Vic gave a little pull on Em's hand. If there wasn't going to be any ice cream he didn't want to stay here, especially if Jessie was going to start asking the same old grown-up questions. He knew from past experience what the next one would be. *How old are you now? Do you like your teacher? What do you want to be when you grow up?* Adults could be so stupid when they talked to children. When *he* grew up, he told himself, he would never ask a kid such silly questions!

Jessie surprised him. "My brother Jerry is in the sixth grade too. Say, our dog Bonnie had puppies recently. When they are ready to leave her why don't you come over and get one? We're trying to find good homes for the litter."

Walking along on Main, out of the brightly lighted section, Vic asked, "Em, do you suppose I *could* have one of those puppies? Handsome is a good dog, but he doesn't run and play with me anymore."

"I know," Em agreed. "He is pretty old."

"Yes, and—Handsome is *Ashton's* dog." He paused. "Are you going to tell Alex when Papa and Ashton will arrive? It sure would be exciting to have the band there at the station to meet them."

"Yes, it would. But I'm not sure Ashton would like it, all that fuss and to-do. And I know Papa would disapprove. He's not one for show."

Both were silent. Only the click of their footsteps on the brick sidewalk broke the quiet of the night. Em tried to quell the twinge of jealousy that seeing Alex and Jessie had brought. Why did she feel this way when she had been trying to think of ways to discourage Alex? Was it his dependability that attracted Jessie? Or had Jessie found in him something exciting that she, herself, had overlooked?

One thing for sure, his quick change of attention had given her own self-confidence a blow. That picture of herself in the library impressing Charlie Hargrove had about as much chance of happening as snow covering the ground in July!

Chapter 9

Patient in the Parlor

Two days later, on Friday morning, Mama received a terse telegram:

RETURNING SATURDAY NOON TRAIN STOP HAVE AMBU-
LANCE AT STATION STOP MOVE ASHTON'S BED TO PARLOR

MAYLEN

Em stood nearby as her mother read the message aloud. "Mama! His bed in the parlor?"

Her lips in a straight line, Mrs. Dudley folded the telegram and put it in her apron pocket. "He must be worse off than we thought. Call Vic in. He can help us move the furniture around in the parlor to make room for the bed."

The rest of the day was a busy one. Em pushed back the sliding doors leading from the hall into the parlor and those leading from the parlor to the sitting room. The parlor was closed off, except on special occasions.

"I know just why Maylen wants him downstairs," Mama said. "He wants us to be able to hear him from our bedroom at night."

Em and Vic pushed one end of the organ as Mama took hold of the other. They shoved the instrument against the wall.

"Now, with the organ out of the way we can put the head of the bed over there and be able to get around the foot," Mama said. "Suppose you take those two footstools out to the sitting room, Vic. Come on, Em, we'll go upstairs and take down the bed."

By suppertime the parlor had been turned into a bedroom and the two sets of sliding doors were closed again.

Saturday morning Em made all the beds and dusted while Mama worked in the kitchen, cooking all of Ashton's favorite dishes that she could think of: marble cake, raspberry pie, soft ginger cookies, potato salad, chicken and noodles, and apple sauce flavored with clove and cinnamon.

Em telephoned again about the ambulance to be sure it would meet the train. Mama said she would not go to the station, but that Em and Vic should drive Prince there just in case the doctor might want to come home ahead of the ambulance.

At eleven-thirty Em and her brother fastened Prince to the station hitching rack and went inside to wait. Shortly after they had seated themselves on a bench there was the noise of much loud talking and laughing outside. Vic stood up and looked through the window.

"Gosh, Sis, it's the town band!"

Em jumped up. Sure enough, there was the band, resplendent in gold-braided red coats and caps, the sun a blinding reflection on their brass instruments.

How had they known Ashton was coming on this train? Em wondered. She had told no one, thinking that if Ashton was sick enough for an ambulance he was too sick to have a band meet him. She saw Alex and went out to speak to him, Vic following.

Alex grinned broadly as he saw them approach. "So you came down too, did you, Em? I guess there'll be quite a crowd by the time the train gets in." Alex tucked his cornet under his arm.

"Of course, I'd be here. Who found out he was coming in on this train?" Em asked.

"Oh, the judge told everybody yesterday afternoon. I think the mayor and City Council will be here soon. We're going to give Charlie Hargrove a real hero's welcome." Alex nodded with satisfaction.

"Charlie Hargrove!" Em exclaimed. "Is he the reason for the band?"

"Why sure, who else could it be?"

"Papa is bringing Ashton home on that train. I think he must be pretty sick. Papa telegraphed to have the ambulance here. There, it's driving up now."

"Oh, golly, Em, I'm sorry. Is there anything I can do?" Alex asked soberly.

"I guess not. You'll be tooting a tune for Charlie when the train gets in. There are the judge and Mrs. Hargrove now getting out of their carriage."

The station platform filled up fast in the next few minutes. The band lined up facing the tracks, the mayor and council members standing in front with the judge and his wife. Em and Vic left Alex and walked to the ambulance. The driver nodded to Em.

"I figure if your brother needs the ambulance he's pretty sick and Doc will probably have him in the baggage car where he can lie down, so I drove up here where they unload the baggage. Quite a crowd down there for Charlie Hargrove. I guess he was wounded in the war."

"Yes," Em answered, wanting to add that Ashton had saved him. But she mustn't resent this big welcome for Charlie; he probably deserved the recognition and if Ashton weren't so sick she probably would be down there with the rest of them, waiting for a glimpse of Harper City's one Rough Rider. Would he have on the uniform he had worn in the picture?

A whistle interrupted her thoughts; the noon train was on time. The driver tightened his grip on his horse as the noisy locomotive steamed past a short way and stopped. The horse stomped and the band started up with a loud blare.

Em looked up and saw Papa standing in the open door of the baggage car. He nodded to her and glanced at the ambulance. A red-coated figure brushed past her and, to her surprise, she saw Alex run to the car and lift himself up beside Papa.

She watched as the ambulance driver handed up the stretcher to Papa and Alex. She gave a little gasp and put her hand over her mouth as a slight, blanket-covered figure was lowered gently from the car. Surely that couldn't be Ashton! The bony, saffron-colored face bore no resemblance at all to her handsome brother.

She stepped forward, only half-aware of the martial music and hurrahs nearby. The closed eyes opened briefly and looked up at her from deep caverns, the lips gave a suggestion of a smile, and then formed the words, "Emmy Lou." It *was* Ashton, but only a shadow of him. Em touched his shoulder and smiled back, controlling her tears with great effort.

Alex, Papa and the driver got the stretcher into the ambulance. Papa turned to Em. "I'll ride in the ambulance with Ashton," he told her. "Thank you very much for your help, Alex. What in tarnation is all that racket going on down there?" he asked.

"It's a welcome home for Charlie Hargrove," Alex explained.

"The devil you say!" The doctor looked at the crowd and the tooting band. Em looked too and saw Charlie standing on a baggage wagon, and he *was* wearing his uniform and the jaunty, one-side-turned-up hat of the Rough Riders. The doctor shook his head in disapproval and got into the ambulance.

Alex followed Em and Vic to their buggy and untied Prince as they climbed up to the seat.

"Thank you, Alex," Em said, taking the reins from around the whip socket. "It was very thoughtful of you to help Papa."

"Let me know, Em, if you need me for anything. I'd like to help Ashton. Now that I won't be able to enlist for the war I figure helping a soldier who was there would be the next best thing. And certainly Charlie Hargrove doesn't need me; the whole town is concentrating on him."

The doctor and ambulance driver were carrying Ashton up the porch steps as Em and Vic drove in. By the time Prince was in his stall and the two were in the house, Ashton had been put to bed in the parlor.

In the kitchen Papa was washing his hands at the wash bench. Mama dried her eyes, blew her nose and spoke in a controlled voice. "Maylen, he's nothing but skin and bones. What can we do for him? Shall I fix a tray for him now?"

The doctor dried his hands then looked at the cake and pies on the table. "In about an hour he can have some broth, nothing else."

"But Maylen!" Mama exclaimed. "I've fixed all the things he likes best, potato salad, stewed chicken and noodles. From the looks of him he needs good food and lots of it."

"Maybe so, in time, but not all this heavy stuff today." The doctor went to the stove and lifted a kettle lid. "I want you to put some of this chicken broth in a pan, let it cool, then skim all the fat off the top. Boil a little barley in it, then strain it. We'll have to feed him, he is too weak to hold up his head."

It was after one o'clock when the Dudleys sat down to dinner. Vic was the only one who did justice to the meal. Em could only swallow a few bites of chicken. She kept remembering Ashton at the table, laughing, talking, and eating heartily of all these tasty dishes.

Papa left his place to telephone Dr. Freetag, asking him to come over later and have a look at Ashton. Returning to the table the doctor said, "I'm going down to my office. Now, listen! One of you look in on him every hour; if he's sleeping, don't disturb him. Give him a cup of that broth about every two hours if he is awake. The train ride was awfully hard on him, but I had to get him home. He wasn't getting proper care where he was." He turned to Vic. "Son, don't make any unnecessary noise in the house or outside. Understand?"

"Sure, Papa," Vic answered, his mouth full of raspberry pie.

"Anything special I can do, Papa?" Em asked.

"Not today, Emmy. When he's stronger you might read to him, an entertaining book of some sort that will take his mind off the things he's been through. A librarian should be able to choose just the right book for a convalescent."

It was a strange, unreal day, Em thought later, as she tiptoed through the hall and peered through the small opening between the parlor doors. He was still asleep. How the strange color of his face contrasted with the white pillow slip! That color must be why they called it yellow fever. Would Ashton ever be himself again? His arms were on top of the coverlet. There was no flesh on his hands at all; the tapering fingers were almost like claws. Em stifled a sob, remembering all that those hands had done for her.

She went out on the front porch and sat down. It was a warm Indian summer afternoon. The leaves on the maple tree were still green. The first frost would bring the brilliant colors Ashton loved so much. She was glad he had come home in time to enjoy autumn. Maybe he would be well enough so that they could celebrate their October birthdays together. Ashton's was October 27 and hers October 25; Mama had often made the twenty-sixth a special day for both of them.

She went down the steps and into the yard; bending down she pulled a weed growing near Blitzen's base. "He's home, Blitzen," she whispered to the iron deer. "Ashton is here again." She closed her lips firmly. She must get over the childish habit of talking aloud to herself. If anyone were near enough to see her lips move they would think she was crazy.

If only it were long ago and she and Ashton were astride Blitzen again and could ride off into the magic land Ashton had been so good at inventing. She could close her eyes and see the places Blitzen had taken the two of them, places abounding in candy trees and cookie bushes, satin-clothed princes and princesses, stone castles and moats, ladies-in-waiting and knights in gleaming armor. How very real he had made their pretend land.

Often she had tried to revive the adventures for Vic, but either her storytelling was at fault or Vic's imagination was lacking, for somehow Vic was never able to really see the fanciful scenes. Vic wanted factual things that really could happen. Perhaps when Ashton was better he would tell Vic some of the wonderful stories he used to tell her.

A click of horse's hoofs brought her back to reality. A carriage stopped at the curb. Em wondered if she might not still be in a fairy tale, for there, alighting from the carriage, was Charlie Hargrove, Rough Rider uniform and all! She walked to the gate and opened it.

Hat in hand, he crossed the sidewalk and smiled at her. "Em, Alex Thompson stopped by our house a few minutes ago and told us that Ashton came home on the noon train too, and that he's very sick. I came right over."

"Yes, Ashton is recovering from yellow fever." The gate swung shut behind them and Em led the way to a bench under the maple. "Won't you sit down? Papa put him to bed in the parlor so we could take care of him more easily. I'm afraid we might disturb him if we sat on the porch."

"Do you think I could see him?" Charlie asked as he sat beside her.

"No. Papa won't even let any of *us* go in except to feed him." Em noted Charlie's healthy tan, so different from Ashton's wasted face. "You are looking well," she added.

"I'm one of the lucky ones," he answered thoughtfully, looking down at the polished shoes below his leggings. "My wounds didn't amount to much, but I could have bled to death if it hadn't been for Ashton. He was right there when I needed him, otherwise I'd have lost my arm. What do you think I can do for him now?"

"Nothing, I'm afraid, except pray. Papa says his recovery will be a long slow process and that quiet, sleep, and proper food are his best medicines. It was nice of you to come over when I am sure your parents still have a lot to say to you."

"I was just thinking, Em, how ironic it was having that big to-do for me at the train, when it was Ashton, there in the baggage car, who deserved the ovation. Yellow fever is a lot more dangerous than a bullet wound." He turned his deep blue eyes to hers. "Em, you've grown up while I was away. What's happened to our class of '98?"

Em told of the various pursuits of the classmates she knew about.

"And what have you been doing besides growing more beautiful?" he asked with a grin.

"So, Charlie Hargrove, that's what you learned in the army! A great way with flattery!" She laughed. "I'll have you know, sir, that I am learning to be a librarian and when the new library opens, I'll be there to see that you get your books back on time!"

"A librarian, hmmmm." He looked at her critically. "I wonder now; you don't resemble Miss Buchanan at all. I thought all librarians wore glasses, the nose kind like hers. But a beautiful creature like Em Dudley? Never!" He crossed his knees and hung the felt hat on his foot, twirling it round and round on the toe of his shoe.

"Jessie Overstreet is going to work in the new library too. Remember her?"

"Slightly."

"Well, you will when you see her. She has grown into the most beautiful girl in Harper City."

"Looking at you, I don't believe it!" Charlie took his hat and stood up. "I've got to go, Em. Father promised Jake Rhorer at the *News* that I'd come down and talk to him. I expect Father told Jake I would describe how I won the war. I've got to get down there and convince him that I had a little help. I understand Father has been bragging about my exploits all over town. I'll have to set Jake straight." They walked toward the gate. "We have a telephone now, Em," he went on. "Will you give me a call when I can see Ashton? Ashton is such a fine fellow, so strong; inside, I mean. Even with all my training under Colonel Roosevelt, now that I'm home I feel pretty much of a kid." He went through the gate and Em closed it.

She looked up at him. "Well, no matter how you feel,

Charlie, you certainly look like a man in that uniform. What do you plan to do now?"

"I'm going to work in Father's law firm for a year. Then if it still appeals to me, I'll enter college and study law."

Em watched him untie the horse from the hitching post. Seated in the carriage, he tipped his hat. "Remember, let me know when he's well enough to see me."

Em nodded and watched the carriage disappear down the street. Heaving a deep sigh, she walked toward the porch. Would Charlie seem as handsome in ordinary clothes? What a mischievous gleam he had in his eyes! As a young boy, he had been a great tease, she remembered. A beautiful creature, he had called her! He still must be a big tease to have said such a thing.

Annoyance at Alex's interest in Jessie was forgotten.

By Sunday evening the entire neighborhood had learned of Ashton's return and by Monday ladies were knocking on the back door to deliver napkin-covered dishes for the soldier, home from the war.

"We have so much food," Em told Miss Buchanan on Tuesday morning, "that Mama doesn't have to do much cooking. Papa won't let Ashton have anything but strained soup and custard, so the rest of us eat the neighbors' donations."

"How is Ashton?" the librarian asked. "I'd like to see him when he is able."

"Papa won't let any of us talk much to him. We just attend to his needs and leave him. He sleeps most of the time. His dog, Handsome, lies in the hall by the parlor door all the time. When any of us take anything in, we have a hard time keeping Handsome out. I'll be glad when we can let him in. Such devotion should be rewarded."

"A box of children's books arrived yesterday," Miss Buchanan said. "The ones purchased with the strawberry-festival money. I wondered if you would like to type up some slips to paste in each one saying it is the gift of your bicycle club."

"That would be nice, Miss Buchanan. Would you mind if I wait until I contact the other members to find out how they would like it worded?"

"All right. You can type them on Thursday. The way things look now, Emmy Lou, we'll be in the new building in less than three months."

Em looked at the calendar on the wall. "Today is September 20. Do you think we'll be in before Christmas?"

"Yes. Possibly we can have our dedication ceremony sometime during the first week in December. I would like to get the moving done in November, hopefully before the snows come. We must not get any of the books wet."

Em looked around. "Have you planned how the books should be moved?"

Miss Buchanan picked up a pencil and absent-mindedly tapped her desk with it. "Well, the Library Board has suggested we hire a moving van. But I want something more dramatic, something Harper City citizens will never forget. I'm thinking of asking the school children to move the books."

"School children! But they will be—" Em stopped. She was going to say children would be more bother than help, but she held her tongue as Miss Buchanan went on.

"Oh, I know a van would be easier, but sometimes things that are more trouble pay off in the end. Now there are fourteen school buildings. We would assign certain days to each school; the grades would come with their teachers and each child would carry a few books down the street to the new library. There one of us would give the class a tour of the building ending in the auditorium, where the children would sit down and hear a short library talk. So, by the time all the books were moved, every child in Harper City would not only have visited the new building but also have had a part in making it into a library. In ten years or so these children will be our adult borrowers. They'll take greater pride in the library if they have a part in its beginning. What do you think?"

"How will we get the books on the right shelves? With all those children plopping them down helter-skelter, it's likely to be—"

"Organization beforehand will take care of that. The children will line up two by two and we'll pass out the books in order. I was thinking that perhaps your club would want to help by seeing that each child's books are put in the right place. I would coach your girls on how I want it done. Do you think they might agree to do it?"

"I think so. We haven't done anything really worthwhile since that strawberry festival. In fact we haven't done much at all, except a couple of picnics out at the park."

After twelve, on Main Street with Miss Buchanan, Em tried to imagine lines of children walking along this way, moving the book collection to the new library. It might work, but knowing that children did not always behave as adults expected, she wondered.

Chapter 10

Teddy Roosevelt Dudley

Late that afternoon Em picked up the evening newspaper from the front steps, unfolding it as she sat in a chair on the porch. Headlines on the front page caught her attention:

ASHTON DUDLEY AND
CHARLES HARGROVE RETURN

As she scanned the column, she gave a sigh of satisfaction. That nice Charlie! He had set Jake Rhorer straight, indeed! The whole story of Ashton finding Charlie on the battlefield was told, giving Ashton's bravery full coverage. Papa would like this, but would the judge? Charlie's quoted words were modest. He was a man she could admire, and not just because he was so handsome in his uniform. There was more to Charlie than just his good looks, she decided. She went to the kitchen and read the article aloud to Mama.

Mama, chopping cabbage for coleslaw in a wooden bowl on her lap, paused in her work. "Oh, that *is* nice. Wasn't that fine of Charlie to say all those nice things about Ashton? He must be a good boy. I don't know how dependable he is but—say, Emmy, why don't you feed

Ashton his supper and then read that to him? He seems
stronger today."

Em folded the paper, dropped it on a chair and got
Ashton's tray from the pantry.

The minute she entered the parlor she knew he *was*
better. His eyes wide open, there was a hint of a grin
on his lips.

"Emmy Lou Dudley, if you are bringing me more soup,
you can't come in. I've had so much soup that if I ate
a bite of bread there would be a splash that folks could
hear all the way to the Court House." He glanced past
her to the open doorway where Handsome stood wagging
his tail, not crossing over into the forbidden room. Em put
the tray on the stand beside the bed and went back to
shut the door. "Let him come in, Emmy, at least just
while I'm eating." Ashton raised his hand briefly to the
dog. "Come here, old fellow."

The dog gave Em a look to see if she was going to
stop him. When she said nothing he walked slowly into
the room, his plume of a tail waving back and forth. He
put his nose over the edge of the bed.

Ashton lightly rubbed the dog's head. "Good boy,
Handsome. Lie down." The dog stretched out beside the
bed, his nose extended on his front paws, his big eyes
looking up, his tail still moving with pleasure.

"Yes, it's still soup for you, soldier," Em said, placing
a light kiss on his forehead. "But since you are complaining about it, you must be better. Papa will enlarge your
diet no doubt." She pulled a chair to the head of the
bed, spread a large towel under Ashton's chin and across
his chest, and sat down to feed him.

"Did Papa say when I could sit up to eat?"

"No, and until he does, you are lying flat. This is
strained vegetable soup. Mama has had it simmering all

day. It's just what you need to strengthen you. If you eat all of it, I'll read you a piece in tonight's paper."

Ashton sighed in resignation. "I am at your mercy, fair damsel. Let's get at it."

The soup finished, Em reached for a small dish of custard. Ashton eyed the newspaper on the tray. "Hold up on that. I feel so full, I don't think I can swallow it yet. Read me your news item."

Em picked up the paper. She read all of what Charlie had told the editor.

Ashton frowned slightly when she finished. "Charlie gives me too much credit. I only did what any doctor would have done. There were others, many others who were more courageous. Anything there about the war or the troops?"

"A reporter describes an exhibition of bronco busting at Camp Wikoff put on by the Rough Riders. At the end of the piece he says that Colonel Roosevelt is going to run for governor of the state of New York."

Ashton's chuckle was a welcome sound to Em; this was the Ashton she knew. "That Colonel Roosevelt, what an amazing man," he said. "He has the energy of one of those broncos his men are so fond of riding. He'll be governor, no doubt. And I'm sure he won't stop there. His part in the Cuban affair has made him as much a hero to the people as Admiral Dewey. The colonel will probably be elected to any high office he tries for."

As she fed him the custard, Em described Miss Buchanan's plan of having the school children transport the library books.

Ashton swallowed and looked ruminatively at the ceiling. "Jenny Buchanan, what a wonderfully imaginative woman she is, and, at the same time, practical and down to earth." He closed his eyes. "Can't you just see it, Em? Miss

Buchanan leading crowds of children up Main Street to the new library, like the Pied Piper and enticing them through the door of *her* magic mountain. I hope I am up and about by that time. I'd love to see it."

"Well, well, well! What's all this conversation in here!" Dr. Dudley looked in. Handsome rose slowly and walked toward the door, as though anticipating banishment from Ashton's side.

"I'm trying to rejoin the world, Papa," Ashton said. "I feel as though I had been brought back from limbo. I'm beginning to think again." Em put the last spoonful of custard into his mouth. "And say, Doc Dudley, I'm getting an appetite; I must have some solid food tomorrow."

The doctor smiled and winked at Em. "Listen to him, Em. Thinks he can tell me how to prescribe for a patient just because he's read a few medical books. Young man, I'll thank you to remember that I'm the doctor around here." Em got up and put the custard dish on the tray. Her father approached the bed, placed his hand on his son's forehead, then felt his pulse. "There is definite improvement," he said as he sat beside the bed. "But we shall follow the same regime for a few more days, son. You aren't out of the woods yet."

"Yes, Doctor," Ashton said with resignation. "I promise to be a cooperative patient."

"All right then. Right now you close your eyes and take a nap. Out with you, Emmy. You too, Handsome."

The dog's eyes looked up sorrowfully at those of the doctor; then, his tail drooping, he went to his former station outside in the hall.

Em, the tray in her hands, stopped at the door. "I read Ashton some of the paper, Papa. Would it be all right if I started reading a book to him tomorrow?"

"I'd like that, Papa," Ashton put in. "If I'm going to be

able to sleep nights, I need to be awake more in the day-time."

"Well, all right, but only for a short time at first, Emmy." The doctor walked to the door.

"Any special book you'd like?" Em asked her brother.

"Yes, *The Red Badge of Courage*. I read it three years ago. But that was before I knew the meaning of war. And since I had those two encounters with the author, I think I may understand better what he was driving at." Ashton closed his eyes. "Get out, both of you! I feel a nap coming on, and my doctor is such an old tartar, he doesn't want my sleep postponed a minute."

Em laughed happily. How good it was to hear Ashton's teasing tone again.

Next morning, there was a feel of fall in the air as Em walked toward the barn for her bicycle. She paused to pick a yellow aster growing near the fence. She would take a bunch of these to the library tomorrow when she went to work.

On her bicycle, she pedaled off to tell the girls about Miss Buchanan's book-transportation project. As she had predicted, the club members were enthusiastic about help-ing Miss Buchanan. Virginia Miller suggested they have a special meeting and ask the librarian to explain just what she had in mind.

It was ten minutes to eleven by the time Em reached the library. Jessie, seated at the work table back of the desk, smiled across at her.

"Good morning, Em. I'm glad you came in. I was going to leave a message for you with Miss Buchanan. Tell Vic he can come over and choose his puppy whenever he wants to. But if he wants a choice he should come soon; there are just three left."

"I'll tell him. He'll probably come after it today. Where is Miss Buchanan?"

"In the back room unpacking a box of new books."

Em walked to the rear and stood in the doorway a moment. Seated at the table, several stacks of new books beside her, Miss Buchanan was lost in the pages of the one opened before her. Em cleared her throat and the librarian looked up.

"Oh, good morning, Emmy. You've caught me. I unpacked these books and the title of this one attracted me and before I knew it I was reading, and here I am, up to chapter ten. It's one of the children's books on the list you and Jessie prepared. I have never read an adult book that gives a more vivid picture of Shakespeare's England. It is delightful."

"What is it?"

"*Master Skylark* by John Bennett and beautifully illustrated by Reginald Birch. It will hold a child's interest, I'm sure. Best of all, there's no preaching or moralizing in it." The librarian closed the book and rubbed its cover thoughtfully. "You have no idea, Emmy Lou, of the impact *Little Women* and *The Five Little Peppers* have had on this country, and all because the authors were mainly interested in telling a good story. Remembrance of Jo March and Polly Pepper will outlive any remembrance of you and me. *You* liked *Little Women*, didn't you?"

Em laughed. "I would have been tossed out of the Dudley household if I hadn't. Remember, my middle name is *Louisa!* Papa didn't like it at first, in fact he wouldn't have it as my first name. Mama soothed him by putting it second and using Emeline first, after Grandma Dudley. But if she had had her way completely I'm sure I would have been called Louisa May. Would Vic like *Master Skylark?*"

"Oh, I think so. It has adventure, a kidnaping, and all

the flavor and vigorous color of Elizabethan England. You can see how it captured me." She put the book aside.

Em sat opposite the librarian. "I've called on all the bicycle club members this morning and they would love to help with the book-moving."

"Good. I'll meet with them soon and outline a definite plan. I have an appointment with the school superintendent tomorrow morning. Think you can manage to hold the fort here while I am gone?"

"Oh, yes. I was telling Ashton about your plan to have the school children move the books. He was fascinated; he compared you to the Pied Piper leading the children into *your* magic mountain. He hopes he'll be well enough to see the plan in operation."

"Dear Ashton! How is he?"

"Improving, I think. Oh, that reminds me; he asked me to get *The Red Badge of Courage* for him. Papa says I may read aloud to him now."

Miss Buchanan nodded. "Ashton has good taste in literature. I'm proud that I had a part in his growing-up years." The librarian chuckled. "So, he called me the Pied Piper, did he? The little dickens!"

That afternoon Em looked into the parlor and found Ashton awake.

"I got that book this morning. Want me to start reading?"

"Please do."

Em pulled a chair near the bed and opened the book.

"How was Miss Buchanan? Full of plans for the dedication ceremony, I imagine." Ashton folded his hands.

"I told her that you compared her to the Pied Piper. It pleased her."

"I'm glad. Well, begin, please. Let's see what kind of

an out-loud reader you are these days. Being in bed here, I'll fall asleep if you don't keep my attention."

Em laughed. "Well, I think Mr. Crane will have to be mostly responsible for holding your interest." She cleared her throat and began:

The cold passed reluctantly from the earth, and the retiring fogs revealed an army stretched out on the hills, resting.

She read on, glancing occasionally at Ashton, lying very still, his eyes focused on the ceiling. Her mind wandered now and then from the story. This certainly was not the kind of book *she* would read for fun. Mostly it was about how a young man felt about enlisting and whether or not he would be a coward and run when he got into battle. Was this how Ashton had felt? Was that the reason he gave such close attention to her reading?

About forty minutes later, the front door bell rang. Em put a marker in the book. "I'll see who that is. Mama went to the grocery."

Charlie Hargrove's broad smile met her at the door. "I saw your father this morning," he told Em. "He said I could talk to Ashton for a few minutes."

"Come in. He'll be glad to see you." Em decided Charlie *was* as good-looking in civilian clothes as he had been in his uniform. "A visitor for you, Ashton," she announced as she and Charlie entered the parlor.

Hat in hand, Charlie approached the bed. "How are you, Ashton?"

"Coming along, I guess, Charlie. Having a doctor in the house, I'm bound to. And Em here is a good nurse." Ashton motioned to the chair by the bed. "Sit down."

Em took the visitor's hat. "I'll leave you two," she said. "Did Papa say how long you could stay, Charlie?"

"About ten minutes."

In the kitchen, Em found the water bucket empty and took it outside to the hydrant and filled it. As she turned off the faucet Vic came running around the house, a wriggling puppy in his arms.

"Emmy, Emmy! Look! Look what I've got!"

"Vic! What a cunning dog!" Em stroked the little animal's head.

"Where can I keep him, Em? I can't let him stay in the house yet. Mrs. Overstreet said not to; he's not housebroken." Vic held the pup to his face to feel its softness on his cheek. "Isn't he sweet, and see, he likes me already, he's kissing me. May I show him to Ashton?"

"I guess so, for a minute. Charlie Hargrove is in there, but I think it's about time for him to leave. I expect you will have to tie the dog in the barn for a while until he learns that this is his home." She picked up the bucket.

They found Charlie standing in the parlor doorway preparing to leave. "Say, that's a nice dog you have there," he said, stroking the puppy's back.

"He is *my* dog," Vic said, bending his head so the dog could lick his cheek. "See, Ashton." He walked toward his brother's bed.

"Yes, I do see, Vic. And I can see he's very fond of you," Ashton said.

Vic held the dog down for Ashton to touch. At this moment Handsome strolled in, his tail held high and motionless. He put his nose on the bed, sniffed at the pup, then rolled his eyes up at Ashton.

Em laughed. "Oh, for goodness sake, Handsome! You are too old to be jealous. Pat him, Ashton, so he'll know you still love him."

"What are you going to call your dog, Vic?" Ashton asked as he rubbed Handsome's head.

"I was going to ask you for a suggestion," Vic answered, taking his dog up in his arms again.

"Well, how about Dewey? Or Admiral, or maybe even Cuba? All very timely names," Ashton answered.

Charlie stepped back into the room. "Say, how about Theodore Roosevelt, if you really want to be timely?" he suggested.

Vic thought a moment. "I'd like that, but it's too long for such a little dog."

"You could shorten it to Ted or T.R.," Em put in.

Vic looked into his puppy's eyes. "I think," he said slowly, "that his name is going to be Teddy Roosevelt Dudley and I'll call him Teddy for short." He murmured into the pup's ear. "You like that, dog? Do you?" Teddy gave a sharp yap and tried to crawl on Vic's shoulder.

"Well, now that we have that settled," Em stated, smiling, "we must all clear out of here. Ashton, you get a nap before supper. Come on, Handsome, out with you."

She walked to the front door with Charlie. "Thanks for coming," she said. "You are the first guest Papa has allowed Ashton to have."

"Is he going to be all right, Em?" Charlie asked, his face serious with concern. "He's so thin."

"Papa thinks so, if we can keep him from catching anything else. In his weakened state even a cold could be dangerous." She looked up at him. Never had she seen such deep blue eyes.

"Well, if there is ever *anything* I can do for him, let me know, anything at all. Will you do that, Em?" She nodded. "Ashton is one of the finest men I ever met and my list includes Colonel Roosevelt. So you can see how he rates with me."

She watched him proceed down the walk. At the gate

he turned and tipped his hat. With springy steps, she walked to the kitchen to the accompaniment of two words singing in her brain: Charlie Hargrove. Charlie Hargrove.

That night Vic slept in the barn to silence the yaps of Teddy Roosevelt Dudley.

Chapter 11

Under the Umbrella

Wending its way into Harper City, October brought brilliant leaves, a deep blue sky and the tangy odor of bonfires. The days were warm with Indian summer, the nights cool with frosts of autumn.

Em's life was well filled; filled with the library, the bicycle club meetings, reading to Ashton, and helping at Papa's office on Saturdays. But it was not so filled as to crowd out thoughts of Charlie.

The back room at the library was stacked with new books, waiting for the opening of the Carnegie building. Miss Buchanan catalogued the books, Em pasted in the pockets and rules, and Jessie labeled the outsides with call numbers and letters.

The superintendent of schools readily assented to Miss Buchanan's plan for moving the books from the old location. A special committee, composed of a representative from every cultural group in Harper City, worked on plans for the dedication ceremony.

By the end of October it seemed that every person in town thought library, talked library, and worked for library. Miss Buchanan fairly glowed at the attention. Em and Jessie felt themselves a part of the excitement and, instead of just working two mornings a week, both went to the library every day, helping to prepare new books and mending the old ones for the shelves of the imposing structure on North Main Street.

Em was eighteen on October 25. As in years past, she and Ashton would celebrate the next day, the twenty-sixth, the day before Ashton's twenty-fifth birthday.

Papa said there was to be no big to-do; Ashton was not strong enough yet. But he did agree that Mama could make a special birthday cake and that all of them could eat dessert in the parlor with Ashton.

It was raining on the twenty-fifth. Em had worked at the library until four o'clock and now, her umbrella over her head, she was walking home through the wet leaves.

She had just lifted her skirts a trifle before crossing muddy Wabash Street, when a bobbing umbrella came up from behind.

"Mind if I join you?" Charlie Hargrove grinned at her from under his umbrella.

"Oh, hello, Charlie!" She let go of her skirt. "I thought you worked at your father's office until six."

"I usually do. But this is a special day, so he let me off. Why don't you put down your umbrella and walk under mine. It's difficult to talk with you so far away." Em complied and stepped under his umbrella. "Take my arm," he directed, "then we can keep in step." Again Em complied. "How are things progressing at the library?"

"Very well. Miss Buchanan thinks we'll have the dedication ceremony on December fifth. The new building is practically ready now. That will give us all of November to move. We could do it in a much shorter time, but Miss Buchanan has this pet project in mind of having the children move the books." Em liked having her gloved hand tucked in the crook of Charlie's arm. She wished she had put on her best hat this morning instead of this old rainy-day hat. But how was she to know he would appear like this? "Where are you going?" she asked.

"To your house."

"Ashton will be glad to see you."

"I wasn't going to see Ashton."

Em looked up at him, her eyebrows raised quizzically. "No?"

"No. Nor to see Teddy Roosevelt Dudley or Handsome, either." He laughed and leaned down. "I'm on my way to call on Miss Emeline Louisa Dudley because it's her birthday!"

Em flushed as her eyes caught his, then she looked straight ahead, smiling broadly. "How did you know that today is my birthday?"

"Ashton told me last week. He was describing how you two always celebrate on the day between your birthdays. Well, I thought I'd get my greetings to you on the exact day. Happy birthday!"

"Thank you." Em swallowed hard to get the tight lump of excitement out of her throat. Don't get yourself in such a state, Emeline Dudley, she told herself. Remember, this is Charlie Hargrove, lately of Roosevelt's Rough Riders, a war hero, with all the girls in town fluttering their eyelashes at him. This attention doesn't mean a thing. He's just being nice to you because you're Ashton's sister. "Ashton shouldn't have told you," she said. "When one gets to be eighteen it's high time to forget birthdays; they're for children."

"Oh, come off it, Em! Everybody likes to have a little fuss made over his birthday no matter what age. I was eighteen last June while I was in Cuba and I felt quite forlorn with no one there knowing or giving a hoot about my birthday. Mother made up for it, though, when I got home. She had the biggest cake for me you could ever imagine." He laughed. "And there, written on it in red-hots, it said *Welcome Home Birthday Boy*. Ever since I can remember, Mother has put a message on my birthday cake with red-hots, you know, those little round red cinnamon drops. I never intend to get too old to like them on my cake. Pretty childish of me, isn't it?"

"I don't think so," Em said. "It's good to feel senti-mental about one's childhood. In our box of Christmas tree ornaments there are three that Papa had as a boy. As long as I can remember he has insisted on hanging those on the tree himself. And from the look in his eyes as he does it, I know he is seeing his parents around a long-ago tree and himself a boy, full of dreams and ambitions. Re-membering things like that—a Christmas tree, red-hots on a cake—well, it helps soften some of the problems of adult life," Em ended, rather pleased with herself, thinking of such a high-sounding remark.

Charlie laughed. "Are you sure you are just eighteen? You are making some pretty mature observations. Say, here's the new library. Let's go up and look in."

They mounted the steps and Charlie put down the umbrella. Pressing their faces against the glass doors, hands cupped on either side, they peered into the marble-walled, lower lobby.

"It's almost too dark to see anything. That dark thing on the wall straight ahead is the bronze plaque. They just put it up last week," Em told Charlie.

"What does it say?"

"'Presented to Harper City, Indiana, by Andrew Car-negie, 1898.' Can you imagine giving such a gift! Just think, being able to give a present to so many people! With it opening in December, I guess we can all count it as our best Christmas present."

Charlie raised the umbrella again, and they walked on,

reaching her home all too soon. She withdrew her hand from his arm.

"Got time to walk around the block?" he asked.

Em glanced up at the house. The front rooms were dark, but lamplight shone from the kitchen. Mama was out there preparing supper and she should be there too, helping. The corner street light came on.

"Well, all right," she answered. Putting her hand back in the crook of his arm, they proceeded to the corner and turned on Oak Street, the raindrops making a sharp tattoo on Charlie's umbrella.

At half-past five they were back again at the Dudleys' gate, walking slowly to the porch and up the steps. Em put her hand on the door knob.

"Oh, wait a second," Charlie said, taking a package from under his arm. "I've got something for you."

Em took the wrapped box he held out. "Just a little something for your sweet tooth," he added.

"Oh, thank you, Charlie. It's very thoughtful of you."

"Oh, think nothing of it. It's a pleasure to give candy to Ashton's sister."

When he had gone she went inside, opened her umbrella and left it to dry. The lamp on the hall table had been lit. She spread her damp coat on a chair and walked dreamily up the staircase, the box of candy held in both hands.

In her room she lit a lamp and then took the paper off the box. Oh, my! Lowney's Chocolate Bonbons! Imagine, Charlie giving *her* Lowney's! Had he given this to her because she was Em Dudley, or because she was Ashton's sister? That was a good question, but they had had that delightful walk in the rain. Surely he wouldn't have suggested that extra walk around the block if he hadn't enjoyed her company. She put the box on the dresser and looked at herself in the mirror for a few minutes, then went to the shelves in the corner and selected a book. She took it to the dresser, put it down beside the lamp, and opened it to the back where a picture postcard marked a place.

This was it, a passage she loved to read over and over. Just now, walking under Charlie's umbrella had reminded her of it, the chapter in which Jo March and Professor Bhaer walked beneath an umbrella, and the beautiful love scene that followed.

Never, never would she outgrow *Little Women,* not even if she lived to be a hundred! How provoked she had been at the author when Jo rejected the proposal of the light-hearted Laurie, but this chapter had helped ease the disappointment. Later books by Miss Alcott showed that the professor was exactly right for unpredictable, tempestuous Jo, and Amy so right for Laurie.

She read the passage to the end of the chapter, gave a long sigh and closed the book. Again she looked at herself in the mirror. There were times when she wished Mama had put her foot down and in spite of Papa's protest had named her Louisa May.

She washed her hands, tucked in a few hairpins, and blew out the lamp. The clock struck six as she descended the stairs.

The next evening Ashton's parlor bedroom was bright with the light from two lamps and the flickering flames of birthday candles on an enormous cake.

"If it is for two birthdays, it has to be twice the size of an ordinary cake," Mama had said.

Papa let Ashton have three pillows under his head while he ate some cake. Em occupied a special chair beside the bed. The pieces of cake eaten, Vic took the plates and forks to the kitchen. Em opened her box of bonbons and passed it around and Mama brought in some presents. There was a taffeta shirtwaist for Em, a shirt and necktie for Ashton, a book of poetry for Em, a book on medicine for Ashton.

Ashton looked up at his father. "You must think I'm going to be up soon, Doctor, and getting back to my studies." He touched the book on the bed.

"Of course, son," Dr. Dudley answered.

Em watched them look into one another's eyes. Was there something the two of them knew that she did not? Ashton *was* better. He ate well and was able to be propped up for an hour or so each day to read. But—he remained thin; he had been home for more than a month. Shouldn't he be out of bed by now, at least part of the time? She tried to disregard a gnawing pain in her throat. He *would* be up and about most anytime now; Papa would see to that!

She passed the candy around again and pretended not to notice that Vic took three pieces. When the candy was all gone, she decided, she would use the beautiful box for her treasures.

The old library on the square was closed to the public all of November. The big move began at two o'clock on Tuesday, November 1. The sixth grade from Washington School gathered in front of the building. Miss Buchanan was everywhere, bustling in and out, giving directions while Em and Jessie handed books to the children. At last they were ready to move.

Jessie closed the door and Em locked it. They stood at the back of the line, Miss Buchanan and the teacher at the front.

"Now remember," Miss Buchanan said to the children. "You must keep your place in line or the books you are carrying will be out of order when you put them on the shelves in the new library. Do you understand?"

"Yes, Miss Buchanan," they answered in unison.

"This is a great occasion," the librarian told them. "When you are grown and take *your* children to the library, you can tell them that you carried the first books into the new building on November 1, 1898. Well, come along. We are off to open the door to the magic mountain!" Miss Buchanan looked at Em over the heads of the children and smiled. Em smiled back and watched the tall, sharp feather on Miss Buchanan's hat bob up and down in rhythm with her firm steps as she led the way up Main Street.

Shopkeepers stood at their doors, drivers in the street stopped their horses, and shoppers paused along the edge of the sidewalk to watch the procession.

"She really is a Pied Piper," Em said to Jessie.

"A Pied Piper?"

Em explained what Ashton had said.

"How is Ashton?" Jessie asked.

Em's smile disappeared. "I don't really know, Jessie. He eats rather well, sleeps a lot, but still he isn't able to sit up but just a short time each day. Papa had Doctor Freetag in yesterday to look him over. He's been home more than a month and still he has that awful color and is just as thin."

"I'm so sorry," Jessie said sympathetically.

Arriving at the steps of the new library, the book brigade was halted by the librarian. On the sidewalk across the street, a big camera was set up, and beside it stood Mr. Hartsook, the town's leading photographer.

"Miss Buchanan," he called out, "hold them there a minute. Jake wants me to get a picture."

The editor of the *News* crossed over and spoke to Miss Buchanan. For a moment Mr. Hartsook stuck his head under the black cloth draped over the camera. "Will you two ladies at the end of the line move in a little closer?" he called out.

"He means us, Jessie," Em said. She straightened her shoulders and lifted her head. She must look dignified for this historic picture.

The picture taken, Em mounted the steps and held the door open. Miss Buchanan led the children inside. The bicycle club girls, having been thoroughly instructed, stood near the shelves and the children deposited their books according to plan. According to plan? Not quite! Two boys pushed and scuffled to get to the shelves first, dropping their books in the fray. Miss Buchanan and the teacher yanked the culprits out of line and shook them vigorously.

Order restored, the librarian took them on a tour of the building, finishing in the auditorium on the second floor. The children sat in the front rows, Em and Jessie and the bicycle club members toward the back. Miss Buchanan began telling how the library got started in Harper City way back in 1877.

As she progressed, Em began to wonder just how interested the children really were in what happened so long ago. All of a sudden a paper wad sailed across the room and landed on the broad brim of the librarian's hat.

Miss Buchanan frowned. "That will be enough of that, Mat Watson! You pay attention or you'll get a paddling!"

The librarian continued speaking on library history, and there were no more paper wads aimed at her bobbing feather. The children were restless but made little noise.

When the children had gone, Miss Buchanan spoke to the club members. "Thank you, girls," she said picking up her coat from a seat. "This went off very well. Now tomorrow there will be two classes in the morning and two in the afternoon. Can all of you be here?"

Virginia Miller stood up. "We think so, Miss Buchanan. At least there will be enough of us to see that the books get in the right places."

"Do any of you have suggestions for making these visits more meaningful to the children?" Miss Buchanan asked as she put on her coat.

No one spoke. Em wondered if the others thought as she did, that Miss Buchanan had kept the children listening too long to library history. What did the children care how many books the library had in its collection in 1880!

Em cleared her throat. "Miss Buchanan, do you suppose the library history part could be made shorter?" she said courageously. "And maybe you could talk about some children's books they might want to read."

The librarian looked thoughtful and pursed her lips. "That may be a good idea, Emmy." She laughed. "When I get started on the early days of the library, I have a tendency to get carried away. I expect I sounded very pompous, indeed, to those children. I'll see what I can do tomorrow to make things more interesting. Thank you.

"Now I'll let you girls in on some wonderful news. Mrs. Albert Wilson, president of the Art Club, made a trip to Indianapolis last week. She has arranged for us to have an exhibit of Indiana artists for our opening week."

"Where will the paintings be hung?" Jessie asked.

"Come along and I'll show you." The girls followed Miss Buchanan across the corridor and through the big double doors. "Right in here will be a fine place to show them off to advantage, with light on two sides. This is the room in which I plan to house a museum eventually."

The next day Miss Buchanan *did* make things more interesting for the children. Seated in the auditorium beside Jessie, Em listened expectantly and watched as the librarian, standing in front, pulled a long hatpin from her broad-brimmed hat and then carefully removed the hat, placing it behind her on the stage.

She smiled at the children. "How many of you have ever read anything in the *St. Nicholas Magazine?*" A few hands went up. "Well, when this library is opened you will always find it on a table in the children's room. I expect some of your parents are familiar with the magazine, for it has been published for twenty-five years and its editor is Mary Mapes Dodge who wrote the book *Hans Brinker or the Silver Skates.*"

The teacher stood up. "Miss Buchanan, I'm reading that book aloud to the boys and girls right now." The children nodded their heads in agreement.

"That's fine," the librarian continued. "Well, Mrs. Dodge not only knows how to write a good story, but she also knows how to select the stories of other authors to put into *St. Nicholas.* Last year she began publishing some excellent animal stories by an author named Rudyard Kipling. They are funny stories and tell how the animals came to be just so. In a recent issue there is one called 'How the Rhinoceros Got His Wrinkly Skin.' I'm going to tell it to you this morning."

Em watched the children lean forward eagerly as Miss Buchanan clasped her hands and began in a low, intimate tone. "Once upon a time, on an uninhabited island on the shores of the Red Sea, there lived a Parsee man from whose hat the rays of the sun were reflected in more-than-oriental splendour."

Jessie nudged Em and whispered, "Oh, isn't she good!"

Em nodded and, as the story unfolded, smiled again and again at the amusing words and phrases, repeated often to create the appropriate folk-tale flavor.

How did Miss Buchanan manage to make those phrases

fall from her tongue so glibly? The children giggled at the often repeated line about the Parsee's hat, from which "the rays of the sun were always reflected in more-than-oriental splendour." And as she told of the Rhinoceros unbuttoning his skin to remove it to bathe, they laughed with glee.

When she finished they applauded enthusiastically. Miss Buchanan reached up on the stage, picked up her hat, put it on her head and jabbed the hatpin through the crown. The children watched expectantly.

The librarian grinned. "Well," she said, "this is *my* hat from which—" She stopped and nodded to the children.

Fairly shouting, the children repeated in unison, "—the rays of the sun are always reflected in more-than-oriental splendour!"

"Good, good! Mr. Kipling himself would be proud of you. Now, if there are any of you who do not have library cards, get a slip at the door, have it filled out at home and bring it back when the library opens."

The children gone, the librarian spoke to Em and Jessie. "Em, your suggestion was a good one. I'm sure that today's class will remember the Parsee man's hat far longer than yesterday's group will remember the library history."

"Miss Buchanan, how on earth did you remember all those unusual words?" Em asked.

"Memorized them. A story like that would lose its charm without the author's exact phrasing. Most stories one tells as one remembers, but not Mr. Kipling's. Now how about each of you girls preparing a story to tell? Suppose you tell one tomorrow, Jessie, and Em, your turn will be the day after tomorrow."

"The only story I know well enough to tell is 'Cinderella,'" Jessie said hesitantly. "I expect I've told that to my sisters a hundred times."

"That will do nicely. 'Cinderella' is always new. How about you, Emmy Lou?"

"I think I'll look in the back numbers of *St. Nicholas* and see if something appeals to me. I'll go back to the library with you later this afternoon and look through them."

That evening, after supper, Em read aloud to Ashton and Vic a Kipling tale she had found in an 1897 issue of *St. Nicholas*, a tale called "How the Whale Got His Tiny Throat."

"That's delightful, Em," Ashton said when she finished. "Imagine a man who could write a serious novel like *The Light That Failed* being able to write a humorous story like that for children. He's a genius, a real genius."

Later, in her room, Em read the story again and again, trying to memorize the phrases and words that gave the tale its charm.

In bed she whispered to herself, "In the sea, once upon a time, O my Best Beloved, there was a Whale, and he ate fishes." She told herself the entire story. She would need to refresh her memory again tomorrow.

She tried to picture herself there in the library's auditorium, telling this story to the children. Would they listen to her? She smiled to herself, thinking of how Miss Buchanan had used her own hat to emphasize her story. She wondered if she, herself, could remember this tale. Would she get frightened and forget?

She must stop worrying and think of something else.

Her walk in the rain with Charlie! How delightful it had been! Under his umbrella, they had seemed in a world of their own. But she had not seen him since and there were so many girls in town; he probably called on a different one every day. But did he take the others boxes of Lowney's Bonbons?

She imagined a scene in the library auditorium. She was telling a story to a huge audience of children. Right in the middle of the tale she looked up and saw Charlie slip in and take a seat at the back. He watched and listened admiringly, and laughed with the children as she repeated again and again Mr. Kipling's words, "You must not forget the suspenders, Best Beloved."

Em turned over and smiled, repeating sleepily, "O Best Beloved! O Best Beloved!"

Chapter 12

"*You* Are the Library"

As the gray November days slipped by, the shelves of the Carnegie building filled up with books. By December every book had been moved, every pupil in Harper City had had a part in the moving and a tour of the new library.

Em had repeated "How the Whale Got His Tiny Throat" so often she was sure she could say it backwards, and "Cinderella" had been told so many times that Jessie said she was sure the pumpkin and mice were hidden somewhere backstage in the auditorium.

On December 1 both girls were put on the payroll of the Harper City Public Library and worked in the building from eight to six, with an hour off at noon. There was so much to do before the opening on Monday. The paintings arrived on Friday and Mrs. Wilson and other Art Club members were on hand to supervise the unpacking and hanging.

Em and Jessie, having brought their lunches, ate quickly and then went upstairs to look at the paintings. After inspecting all of them, Jessie said, "I had no idea we had such talented Indiana artists. Which one do you like best, Em?"

"They all seem good to me, but that one is my favorite,

I believe." She walked to the end of the room where a large painting filled the entire space near the window. Em read the card stuck in the corner of the frame. "It's called 'Autumn in Brown County.' Isn't it lovely?" She stepped back to the door and viewed the picture at a distance. "What warm strong colors!"

"Miss Buchanan said she thought the Browning Club was going to buy this one for the library." Jessie pointed to a landscape near the door.

On Sunday, Reverend Roxberry spoke of the new library in his sermon. "The new library belongs to the citizens of Harper City," the minister said. "It will be open every evening next week for inspection. I hope all of you will turn out to see your new piece of property."

If that sort of announcement was made in every church today, Em thought, they would have crowds of visitors next week. And she was sure the school children had spread the news of their visits. Miss Buchanan had said, "If you want a good idea to take hold, enlist the interest of the children."

Now the minister veered back to the subject of his sermon and Em's mind wandered. Papa had stayed home with Ashton this morning so the rest of them could come to church. How she wished Ashton could go to the dedication ceremony tomorrow evening. Em had described to him every room in the building. She could see his dear gaunt face now, his eyes burning bright with interest as she answered his many questions.

Most people seemed to have forgotten last summer's war, but the Dudleys could not. Ashton's condition was a constant reminder. Em had read that 514 soldiers had died of disease in Cuba and half again as many at Montauk. Was Ashton dying right there in the parlor? Dying in spite of all they could do? Tears welled up in the corners

of her eyes. She wiped them away quickly so Mama
wouldn't see. What a price to pay for the annexation of
the Philippines and for Cuba's freedom from Spain! And
now there were reports in the paper about the United
States acquiring the Hawaiian Islands. It seemed to Em
that Ashton was paying for all of it, even the election
in November of Colonel Roosevelt as Governor of New
York. Papa said the colonel had been elected because of
the publicity gained while he had been Lieutenant Colonel
of the Rough Riders.

And Charlie Hargrove, what about him? Em found it
difficult to blame Ashton's condition on Charlie. But what
had become of him? Somehow, after that walk in the rain
on her birthday she had thought he would call on her
again soon. But all of November had gone by and no
sign of him. Perhaps he would be among those visiting
the library next week. How she would like to conduct
him on a tour! She wondered if Jessie felt like this about
Alex Thompson. Em knew that Alex was calling on Jessie every Sunday evening. He must be serious about her.
Since Charlie's return, though, Alex's fickleness seemed
unimportant.

At nine the next morning people began arriving to inspect Mr. Carnegie's gift. Em, dressed in her birthday
shirtwaist and black skirt, was at the charging desk to answer questions and check out books. The people, however, were too interested in the building itself to take time
to select books.

Upstairs, members of the Art Club were on hand to
explain the exhibit. The paintings were for sale; the club
members were ready to give prices to anyone affluent
enough to consider buying. Jessie was stationed in the hall
upstairs and Miss Buchanan circulated among the people
on the first floor. Throughout the day, members of the

H.C.B.C. were scheduled to stand at the front door and hand out souvenir booklets of the library.

Seated on a tall stool behind the charging desk, Em felt every inch a librarian, from the knot of brown hair, which she had coiled on top of her head for added dignity, to the toes of her high laced shoes that she had polished last night to a shiny gloss. She was sure Queen Victoria at her recent Diamond Jubilee had not felt any grander than did Emeline Louisa Dudley at this moment.

This morning, before she left home, she had gone into the parlor for Ashton's inspection.

"Emmy dear, you look beautiful," he had told her.

"But do I look smart enough to be a librarian?" she had returned.

"Not only look smart enough, but you *are* smart enough. I'm very proud of my little sister. Your gold watch pinned on that new shirtwaist gives you quite an elegant air. Wish I could put on my birthday shirt and tie and go down to see you in action. Give Miss Buchanan my greetings and say to her that no matter how fine the library building is or how many books there are on the shelves, to me, *she* is the library." He had looked away then, and thought for a moment. "I expect that's a good thing to remember, Emmy, especially when dealing with children. To every child who faces you across the desk or questions you beside the bookshelves, at that moment to him *you* are the library." Ashton had smiled then and taken her hand. "It seems to me that it takes more than a building or books to make a library." Squeezing her hand at this point he had continued, "Please, Emmy, look at everything twice today, for I shall want a detailed report on all that goes on down there."

Dear, dear Ashton! That was the only flaw in this won-

derful day, that he was not well enough to be here to
see her in this exalted position.

Several times, looking through the glass that shut off
the outer lobby, she thought she saw Charlie going up the
marble staircase to the upper floor. But so far he hadn't
appeared. Where was he? What had he been doing since
October? Not reading law in his father's office all the
time, she was sure. Certainly he would show up in the
new library sometime today. Would she rather he saw her
here behind the desk or outside on the floor, ready to
take him on a tour? She had memorized the titles and
artists of all the paintings upstairs. She felt she would be
a rather good guide; even Charlie might be impressed at
so learned a librarian.

She smiled inwardly. Watch it, Em Dudley! she told
herself. Don't be foolish! You really know practically
nothing about being a librarian!

At eleven-thirty Em ate the lunch she had brought. At
twelve Miss Buchanan closed the library, and she and
Jessie went home, leaving Em in the building.

Now that the library was empty there was only the tick
of the big clock mounted on a panel opposite the charging desk. Em went out the little swinging wooden gate
at the back of the desk area and walked into the reading
room. Returning to the desk with three magazines, she sat
on a low chair and began turning pages. She paid particular attention to continued stories, their titles and authors.
So often these were published later in book form and
it would be important that she know about them.

She looked at the advertisements, extolling everything
from bustles to stove blackening. A column called "Literary
Queries" attracted her attention. One item interested her
especially.

"The appointment by Queen Victoria of Alfred Austin

as a successor to Tennyson as Poet Laureate of England was not a popular one. Had the popular choice been consulted the honor would probably have been bestowed upon Rudyard Kipling."

Em nodded her head in agreement. Of course it should have been Rudyard Kipling! What was the matter with the Queen! Who ever heard of Alfred Austin?

Oh, she *was* feeling superior today! Here she was criticizing the Queen!

The ringing of the telephone in Miss Buchanan's office brought her back to her responsibilities. She hurried across the lobby and through the door to the office. Standing beside the telephone on the wall, she hesitated. Should she just say hello, or—?

Clearing her throat, she took the receiver off the hook and spoke firmly into the mouthpiece. A little tingling thrill crept up the back of her neck as she said, "Harper City Public Library."

"This is Judge Hargrove speaking."

The thrill disappeared and Em's throat grew dry. "Yes, sir."

"I wish to speak to Miss Buchanan."

"I am sorry, she is not here."

"Then who is speaking?"

Em drew herself up tall and took a deep breath. "This is Miss Dudley," she replied in a dignified tone.

"Oh, yes, Emmy Lou. Charles did tell me you were going to work in the library. Well, now, listen. You tell Jenny that I've had word from Bert Long. He has a bad cold and has lost his voice. He asked me to take his place on the dedication program tonight. I have agreed to do it. So you tell Jenny. Have you got that?"

"Yes, Judge, I shall tell her."

"Very well. I'll be there tonight a little early, so I can get the lay of the land."

"Yes, sir."

"Good-bye."

"Good-bye, Judge."

Em hung the receiver on its hook. Well, since the judge was going to be on the program surely Charlie would come to hear his father. She wondered if she should change her clothes when she went home to supper. Perhaps she should wear her green alpaca dress. No, she would keep on what she was wearing. This new waist was becoming and dignified. She felt that it made her look older, perhaps even twenty-one or twenty-two.

Crowds thronged the library all afternoon. Em, stationed on the second floor, took pride in showing the small meeting rooms and the fine library hall. The Art Club ladies were on hand so Em had no opportunity to demonstrate her knowledge of the paintings.

At six, she went home to supper and returned before seven. Mama and Vic arrived shortly thereafter. Mrs. Calhoun, a neighbor, was staying with Ashton. Papa, of course, had gone to his office.

By seven forty-five all seats in the auditorium were taken, the corridor outside was filled, and also the art exhibit room. Em slipped through the crowd into the auditorium and stood in the back.

Seated on the platform were Reverend Elmore, Judge Hargrove, Miss Buchanan, and several others Em did not know. She was to be here for the first part of the program, then go downstairs and stay at the desk while Jessie came up for the last half.

Em looked at the audience, recognizing persons here and there. Suddenly broad shoulders, three rows from the back, caught her eye. Was it—could that be Charlie? The head on the shoulders turned to the young woman in the next seat. It was he! Em moved a bit to the right in order to get a better view. How had she missed seeing him come in? And who was that beside him? Had they come together?

It was only when Judge Hargrove rose to start the program and the young lady removed her hat that Em recognized her. Molly Flannery! Em bit her lip in vexation. So, Molly was the reason Charlie hadn't been around; Molly, a member of the bicycle club, Molly, a friend of hers, Molly, who everyone knew was a flirt of the first water!

The judge was speaking, but Em didn't hear. Maybe they hadn't come together. Maybe it was by chance that they were seated side by side. No, that probably wasn't true, for at this very moment Charlie was helping Molly out of her coat. Em looked away. She must pay attention to the program so she could tell Ashton.

"It is with honorable city pride and with much personal pleasure that we meet beneath the roof and within the walls of this superb structure, devoted, as it is, to literature and the intelligent elevation of the people. A state, a city, a community, commends itself to the intelligence of the outside world by a collection of such books as we hope to see adorning the shelves of this beautiful building." The judge warmed to his subject, calling the library a temple dedicated to raising the educational level of the people to a high plateau of excellence. He spoke of Andrew Carnegie at length, calling him the nation's generous benefactor, and continued in a long eulogy.

Em stepped back and leaned against the rear wall. Here she could not see those two heads, so near one another. She closed her eyes for a moment, and, for the first time today, she felt tired. At last the judge finished his flowery speech and the program continued. There were musical numbers, vocal and violin, then more speeches.

Em left after Miriam Goodpasture sang her solo, and downstairs again, she sat on the high stool behind the desk and relieved Jessie.

It was good to sit. There was not much to do here. Only a few people came up to ask questions. Those not able to get into the auditorium wandered about through the stacks, into the reading room and the children's room.

Em tried not to think of Molly sitting up there beside Charlie, but to no avail. She kept remembering Molly's habit of opening her eyes wide, so that her long dark lashes framed those big black eyes of hers in a look of surprised innocence. Innocence, my eye! Em thought. That Molly knew every trick in the book! Until now Em had always been amused at Molly's coquettish ways. But now, well, if that girl thought she was going to have a clear field with Charlie, she was mistaken. Just maybe, *she,* Em Dudley, had a few ideas on the subject that Molly had never dreamed of!

Dr. Dudley came in at a quarter past nine, and he smiled as he approached the desk. "Emmy, you look great sitting there, as knowing and wise as a, well, as a librarian! How did things go at the dedication?"

"All right, I guess. And it's still going on. I expect Vic is getting sleepy by this time."

"Probably. But I bet your mother is loving every minute of it. You look tired, Emmy Lou. This has been quite a day for you. How soon can you go home?"

"I imagine it will be an hour or so after the dedication is over. Lots of people will want to inspect the rest of the building." Em looked across at the clock. "This program is taking longer than Miss Buchanan had planned."

The doctor smiled. "When Harper City dedicates a library it stays dedicated. Especially if Judge Hargrove has anything to do with it. I tell you what, honey, I want to look in on Ashton, so I'll walk Mama and Vic home, then I'll come back for you."

"Thank you, Papa." Earlier today, a picture had flashed in her mind; Charlie would step up to the desk after the program and ask to take her home. Now, after what she had seen upstairs, she knew that was not to be.

The doctor went upstairs and soon thereafter the crowd began descending the two marble staircases. Em watched and, after a while, saw Charlie and Molly. Molly was talking all the way down the stairs, using her expressive face to full advantage. Charlie appeared to be fascinated. They did not come into the main lobby, but went on down the second staircase and out the front door.

Em swallowed hard. Oh, Charlie, how could you forget so soon that walk in the rain and the Lowney's Bonbons!

A lady approached. "Emeline, can you tell me how many books there are in the library now?"

Em returned to the present. "Right now, Mrs. Riley, we have over nine thousand volumes, and circulation so far this year has been more than thirty-five thousand books. We are getting new books all the time. Miss Buchanan is eager to increase our collection with the best that is being published." Oh, if only Charlie were standing at the desk and could hear her! Surely being a librarian should count for more than dark eyes with curling lashes!

Papa came back for her, Alex Thompson came for Jessie, and Miss Buchanan walked home with her brother and his wife.

Outside it had grown colder, and the crisp air was filled intermittently with small snowflakes, the kind that stung as the wind whipped them against your face.

"Ashton was still awake when I took Mama home. I

expect he's waiting to see you. Mama put Vic right to bed; he was fairly asleep by the time he climbed the stairs." The doctor tucked Em's hand in the crook of his arm. "Is anything wrong, Emmy? You've been uncommonly quiet."

"Guess I'm just tired, Papa." She couldn't tell him that she was jealous of the time Molly Flannery had spent this evening with Charlie Hargrove. How stupid she was! A walk under a cozy umbrella, a gift of candy, and here she was counting Charlie as her own! To divert her father from herself, she asked, "Papa, how is Ashton, really? After those first few weeks, I haven't been able to see any improvement at all."

The doctor did not answer at once, then hesitantly he said, "You are right, honey, he is *not* improving." His voice grew husky as he added, "And he's not likely to."

Em stopped, removed her hand from her father's arm and faced him. "Papa! What do you mean?"

The doctor put his arms about her. "Emmy, you have to know. I can't tell Mama yet and I need your strength to get me through what's ahead. It will be a miracle if he lasts until Christmas."

Em's tired body grew limp as she sobbed on the shoulder of her father's overcoat.

"There, there, Emmy Lou, I'm sorry I had to tell you, but I'll need you to help me prepare Mama. Only three people know," he went on, "Doctor Freetag, myself and —and Ashton, and now with you, that's four."

Em raised her head. "Ashton knows?"

"Yes. I couldn't fool him, he knows too much about disease and medicine. Just now, before I left the house, he asked me to tell you. He said, 'Em's strong, she can bear it, and I want her to get used to the idea before it happens. Then she'll be better able to help Mama.'"

The doctor gently pushed Em away, unbuttoned his over-coat and got a handkerchief from an inner pocket. "Here, honey, dry your eyes."

The two walked on. So, Ashton thought she was strong! Never in all her life had she felt so weak. Her knees were like jelly. If it weren't for Papa's arm she was sure she would fall. But Papa! What about him? She glanced toward him, seeing only the dim outline of his head, his coat collar turned up against the wind.

Compared with Papa's love for Ashton, her own was insignificant. Papa had lived for the day Ashton would set up practice with him and they would work together. Papa's love and pride for his first-born were boundless. Em wondered that he was able to talk to her so calmly of this coming tragedy. Papa had battled death so often and won. How terrible that he was to lose this encounter.

They were silent until they turned in at the gate. "Do you think you can go in and speak to him before you go to bed?" the doctor asked.

Em took a deep breath. "Yes, Papa. If he thinks I'm strong then I'll have to be strong."

He patted her hand. "Good girl."

Inside, the lamp burned in the hall. Em and her father removed their wraps. He pushed back the sliding door and said, "Ashton, here's a young librarian to see you."

"I've been waiting." Ashton's voice was low and clear.

Em looked up at her father. He squeezed her shoulder hard. She walked into the room, dimly lit by the hall lamp.

"Well, how did it go, little sister? Tell me all about it. All Mama told me was that Judge Hargrove almost lifted the roof with his oratory."

Em pushed a stool to the head of the bed and sat down. Papa disappeared from the doorway and she was left with her brother. Her throat ached and her eyes burned. She longed to put her head on the bed and let fly with the tears waiting to be shed. Instead she touched Ashton's hand and said:

"Ashton, you never saw so many people! Just thousands milling through that building all day. And what a crowd tonight! Only half of them could get into the hall."

"And you, Emmy Lou, what did you do?"

She clasped his hand. "I answered ever so many questions. And do you know what? Everytime a patron questioned me I remembered what you told me this morning."

"What was that?"

"You said that when anyone spoke to me, at that moment *I* was the library. It's quite a responsibility you put on me, Ashton. I'm not sure I'll always be up to it."

He squeezed her hand. "Oh, yes, you will. The little girl who used to ride with me on old Blitzen's back never got tired or lacked enthusiasm. No matter how far we rode, you would beg to ride farther. I was always the one who got tired and dismounted first. You are going to be a fine librarian, Emmy dear. Now tell me just what the judge said. And was Charlie there?"

Em took a deep breath and related all she could remember, all except about Charlie and Molly. Ashton thought her strong, and strong she would be, no matter what! She couldn't disappoint such a brother.

But at this moment she could not tell him that she knew his time was short. She was not strong enough for that yet.

In bed, exhausted by the physical and emotional strains of the day, Em sobbed herself to sleep.

Chapter 13

To a Faraway Land

There were moments during the days that followed when Em was so occupied *being* the library to its patrons that she forgot the ache in her chest. But, alone in the work room, pasting pockets in new books or mending old ones, the pain returned with agonizing force. She did not cry but, oh, how she longed to do so! Faced with the approaching tragedy, her thoughts of competing with Molly for Charlie's attention faded into insignificance.

That first week, the library was open every night until nine to give all an opportunity to visit the place. But the following week the regular schedule of hours began, the building being open three evenings, Monday, Wednesday and Saturday. Em's night duty fell on Wednesday. That day she did not go to work until noon.

Other evenings and Wednesday mornings she spent with Ashton, reading to him, talking to him, describing the people she met in the library, re-creating as best she could the outside world for the patient in the parlor.

Christmas came on Sunday and the miracle had happened—Ashton was still with them. They had put the Christmas tree in the sitting room and opened the sliding doors so Ashton could see it.

It snowed Christmas morning and a blustering wind piled drifts against the house. In the sitting room the base-burner glowed with blue flames and yellow coals, while the smaller stove in the parlor became red hot on top.

After breakfast, they unwrapped presents beside Ashton's bed. Handsome showed no interest in the proceedings, preferring to lie in the other room near the base-burner. Vic's pup, Teddy, was everywhere, taking bits of discarded tissue paper in his mouth and running with them, shaking his head and growling at Handsome to show the old dog how fierce he really was. Dropping a piece of paper near Handsome's nose, the little one barked sharply. Handsome opened one eye, then closed it.

"It's no use, Teddy," Em said. "Handsome is just too old to get excited about Christmas. Hush all that barking!" She left the parlor, picked up the noisy pup and returned to her chair.

"Tie a bow on his collar with this red ribbon, Em," Vic said.

Mama smiled and patted Ashton's hand. "Do you remember, son, the Christmas you and Emmy took her box of hair ribbons and tied bows all over Blitzen's antlers?"

"I remember, Mama. I guess old Blitzen has never been that gay since." Ashton looked across at Em.

Vic pulled on the new mittens he had just opened. "Oh, yes, he was. You should have seen him last summer when we had the strawberry festival. There were lighted Japanese lanterns all over his head."

Em folded a piece of tissue paper for future use and placed it in a box. "Our whole yard was lovely that night, Ashton, the lanterns gave a kind of fairy-tale light. I expected to see old Blitzen mount a road right up into the sky and toss his lantern-covered antlers at the moon."

"And Blitzen is just the deer who could do it, too," Ashton returned with a smile.

Vic shook his head. "You two and that deer. He's just an iron statue!"

Em and Ashton exchanged glances. "Not to us, Vic," Ashton said. "Why, he took us to faraway lands you have never dreamed of."

Em leaned down and retied her shoe to hide the tears that stung her eyes.

"Well, I guess we have opened all the presents," Mama said briskly, straightening the quilt on Ashton's bed. "I'll go have a look at the turkey, then I'll get ready for church."

Em watched Mama. There was something in the look she gave Ashton. Could it be that she knew too? Maybe Mama was stronger than either Ashton or Papa thought.

Vic and the doctor put on boots and heavy mittens and went out to shovel paths to the barn and to the street. Em stayed with Ashton, picking up scraps of paper and ribbon scattered about. She put the gifts in the sitting room under the tree.

"Want me to shut the doors so you can take a nap?" she asked him. "You look tired. I expect we dragged out this present-opening business too long."

"No, I want to talk, Emmy. Sit here."

She opened the door of the parlor stove and dropped in some bits of paper, then sat beside the bed.

Ashton looked up into her face. "Papa said that he told you I'm not going to be here very much longer."

Em looked away and said faintly, "Yes." I must not cry! she thought. I must not!

"Now, listen, Emmy Lou. It's not a sad thing at all. At first I was rebellious and asked the Lord, 'Why me?' But now I'm so awfully tired of this bed, it will be a welcome change to leave it. Just think of me as riding off on old Blitzen to one of those lands we used to visit. I told Papa I wanted you to know so you will be able to help Mama bear up afterward. But that wasn't quite true. Papa is the one who will have the hardest time.

I want you to be with Papa as much as you can. He is likely to turn bitter; he has had such plans for me in his office. Bitterness can just eat up a person, Emmy. Help him adjust."

"But how, Ashton, how can I do it?"

"You'll find ways. This year of '98 is almost finished, Emmy. It's been a great year. I'm glad I had a part in it. I expect our country will never be quite the same again. The new century is almost upon us, and oh, Emmy! the wonders you will live to see! Take two looks at everything, one for you and one for me." He took her hand.

Em swallowed hard. "If only you hadn't joined the army!" she blurted out.

"There's a purpose in everything, Em. If I hadn't I could not have been on the spot when Charlie Hargrove needed me. To brag a bit, but for me he would have bled to death or lost his arm. Charlie is a lad worth saving. Don't you agree?" He gave her the boyish grin she remembered so well.

"Yes, but—"

"Keep your eye on Charlie. That boy is going places."

Em nodded and the thought flashed, yes, but with whom? "Ashton, couldn't you and Papa be wrong? You seem so well this morning."

"I think not, honey. Open Bryant's book of poems there at the marker." Em did so. "Now read the portion of 'Thanatopsis' I have underscored."

Em read:

> . . . go not, like the quarry-slave at night,
> Scourged to his dungeon, but, sustained and soothed
> By an unfaltering trust, approach thy grave
> Like one who wraps the drapery of his couch
> About him, and lies down to pleasant dreams.

Em saw the last lines through tears. She closed the book and returned it to the bedside table.

"That's the way I want to go, Emmy, and I'm ready anytime. I'm counting on you to keep things humming in this household. With the interesting life you will lead at the library, you can regale the folks with accounts of it and keep them from gloom."

"Ashton, I'll try." Em knelt and rested her forehead on the bed.

He touched her hair. "I know you will, little sister. Having you has been one of the high points of my life. Now run along, I'm sleepy."

He put his arms under the comforter and Em covered his shoulders. As she kissed his forehead, one teardrop fell. He smiled up at her. "Good girl, Emmy Lou, good girl," he murmured, and closed his eyes.

It was twilight of the same day when the doctor discovered that Ashton had died in his sleep. Outside, the setting sun reflected blue light on the snow; the bare branches on the tree near the parlor window rattled bleakly in the wind.

Em came in with a tray and found her father staring unseeingly out the window. A glance at the bed, where the doctor had covered Ashton's face with the sheet, told her that the time had come.

She put down the tray, slid open the doors to the sitting room, led her father out to a rocker by the base-burner, then closed the doors to the parlor.

Dr. Dudley sat without rocking, still staring into space. Em went to the telephone in the hall and called the Calhouns' number. They were the only neighbors in the block who had a telephone.

"Mrs. Calhoun, this is Emeline Dudley. Could you come? Ashton just left us."

The telephone call made, Em went to the kitchen and quietly told Mama.

"I must go to Maylen," Mama said, her face turning pale.

Ashton was right, Mama *was* the strong one. She must have known all along. Beside her husband in the sitting room, she took his hand and murmured, "Maylen, we knew it was coming. We were lucky to have had such a son for twenty-five years. Not many parents are so blessed."

Em went to the door to let in Mr. and Mrs. Calhoun, also the next-door neighbors, the Brandons, whom the Calhouns had alerted.

After that the evening was a blur to Em. Mrs. Calhoun and Mrs. Brandon took over and managed everything. Oh, how good it was to have such neighbors! Mr. Brandon took the doctor for a long walk through the snow-covered streets. When they started out, Em watched her father being helped into his overcoat. Ashton had been right about him too; Papa's heart was broken. Doc Dudley, a man of iron stamina and strength, had collapsed.

Mama wept softly as she wrote the names and addresses of out-of-town relatives who must be sent telegrams. It was Mama who talked to Mr. Gould, the undertaker, when he arrived, and told him how and where on the Dudleys' cemetery lot Ashton was to be buried. It was Mama who talked to their minister about the funeral. Mama *was* strong. How well Ashton had understood his family.

Em hoped he had been right about herself, but as she got into bed that night she felt anything but strong. It took hours to cry herself to sleep.

At half-past seven the next morning, Mrs. Brandon let

Miss Buchanan in at the back door. Em left the dining room table, where the family was pretending to eat breakfast, and spoke to the librarian in the kitchen.

"I was going to telephone you, Miss Buchanan, at eight, when I knew you would be at the library."

"I just heard, Emmy Lou. Now don't you worry about the library. Your family needs you. How is your mother bearing up?"

"Mama is wonderful. It's Papa who just can't seem to pull himself together. He called Doctor Freetag and asked him to make his house calls. You know he's bad off when he does that."

"Where is he, Emmy? I'd like to talk to him."

"In the sitting room. He wouldn't even try to eat breakfast. Come on, I'll take you to him. But don't be surprised if he is rude. I thought he was prepared for this. Ashton knew. He said it would be this way." Em led the way through the hall and into the sitting room where the doctor sat beside the back window, staring at the snow-covered yard and barn.

Miss Buchanan moved toward him. "Maylen," she said in her firm voice.

Em left them, hoping his old friend could bring Papa around to a semblance of his vigorous, sensible self.

During the morning the neighbors helped Mr. Gould in the parlor. The bed was taken down and returned to Ashton's room upstairs. By noon a coffin had replaced the bed in the parlor.

Only once that morning had Papa spoken. Mr. Gould had come into the sitting room and said, "Doctor, we are ready to dress Ashton. I was wondering if you wanted him dressed in his uniform."

The doctor had jumped up and glared at the undertaker.

"Not by a damn sight! I don't want anything of that hellish war near my boy! Do you hear?"

Em had exchanged glances with Mama, then had taken her father's arm and led him back to his chair. Seated, the doctor had closed his eyes and leaned his head against the chair back.

"Mr. Gould," Mama had said. "You'll find a navy blue suit in Ashton's closet upstairs. That will be the one."

In the afternoon there were two steady streams of visitors at the Dudleys', one at the back door where neighbors brought food for the bereaved family, and one at the front door where friends came to pay respects to the living and to view the dead.

By four o'clock Em felt numb, felt as though she were floating around outside her body, watching herself there in the sitting room being embraced tenderly by sympathetic, weeping ladies and spoken to by somber-faced men. Papa shut himself in the downstairs bedroom and refused to see anyone, leaving Mama and Em to meet the visitors.

At six the dining room table was spread with the donated food. Mama led Papa to his place at the table.

"Where is Vic?" Em asked.

"I haven't seen him all afternoon, Emeline," Mrs. Calhoun said from the kitchen doorway.

"I'll find him." Em remembered that early in the afternoon she had seen her brother climbing the stairs with Teddy in his arms. Upstairs, she paused a moment before the closed door to Vic's room, then went in. The reflection of a half moon on the snow outside threw a dim light around the room. Wrapped in a comforter, holding Teddy close, Vic lay asleep on the bed. The dog roused as Em lit the lamp.

She sat on the bed, patted the dog, then brushed back

Vic's hair. His face was swollen from crying. Poor child, Em thought, no one had paid any attention to him at all up here crying his heart out in this cold icy room.

"Vic, Vic, honey. Wake up. It's Em."

The boy stirred. The dog licked his face and let out a faint yap. Vic opened his eyes.

"It's time for supper, honey. Will you get washed and come down?" Em gave him a smile.

"Oh, Emmy, I'm not hungry."

Em felt his forehead for a fever. Only an illness could take his appetite. "Oh, come on now. You don't feel hot, you're not sick. There are lots of good things down on the supper table."

"I just don't believe I can swallow, Emmy. Seems like my throat's got something big stuck in it."

"I know, mine too. But Mama and Papa need us. You will have to help me comfort them. Ashton counted on you."

Vic threw back the cover and Teddy jumped to the floor. "Do you think so? I tried to talk to Papa this morning. I wanted to tell him what I've decided. But he didn't listen; I don't think he even saw me." There was a catch in the boy's voice.

"You will have to be grown up enough, Vic, to forgive Papa right now. This has hit him so hard. He had counted on Ashton more than any of us. He had planned his whole future with the two of them working together."

"But, Em, that's what I tried to tell him, that I'm going to be a doctor too and help him in his office. But, Emmy, he wouldn't even listen." Vic's eyes sparkled in the lamplight, as more tears gathered.

Em put her arms about him. "Oh, Vic, honey, I'm sorry he ignored you. But just be patient. For the time being you just pretend that you are the father and he is your son.

Just as parents have to be patient with children, there comes a time when children have to be patient with parents. Soon Papa will be himself and welcome your news. You wait and see. Come on now, you eat a little and that lump in your throat will disappear."

It snowed again that night. Em lay awake listening to the icy wind rattle the windows and shutters. A crack of light showed under her closed door from a lamp in the lower hall.

Dear Vic, deciding to be a doctor! When would Papa come to and remember that he had a second son? It might be a long time. Grief was like an illness; in the first stages it fairly consumed its victim. Only time could cure—time and useful work. When Papa remembered how his patients needed him, then perhaps— Thank goodness, she had her library work. How awful for Mama; she would have to stay in this house where memories of Ashton filled every room.

Ashton Dudley was buried on December 27. Charlie Hargrove was one of the pallbearers. When he came to the house for the funeral he had caught Em's eye across the room. Em nodded slightly and noted the suffering in his handsome face. She knew he was thinking that, but for Ashton, he would not be here today.

The sliding doors to the sitting room and those to the hall had been pushed aside, and rows of folding chairs had been set up. The minister stood in the parlor beside Ashton's flower-banked coffin and read Scripture and a long eulogy.

The snow was deep. The casket was put on a bobsled for its trip to the cemetery. The mourners followed, riding in sleighs; the horses wore no sleigh bells.

Mama and Papa walked out the front door together. Em followed, holding Vic's hand.

The afternoon sun cast a brilliant sparkle over the front yard. Em paused a moment at the bottom of the steps and looked out at Blitzen, his antlers tipped with snow. She caught a quick glimpse of a blond boy astride the animal and a small girl behind him, her arms tight about his waist.

"Come on, Em." Vic pulled her hand.

"Yes, Vic."

Ashton was riding off again into a faraway land, but this time she was left behind.

Chapter 14

New Year's Eve

Two days later, Em returned to the library.

"If you'd rather not face the public yet, Emmy Lou," Miss Buchanan told her, "you may do some work in the back room."

"Oh, no. It's all right. I must get used to meeting people, and talking to them about Ashton." Em's eyes filled with tears. "Did you read the wonderful article Mr. Rhorer wrote about him in yesterday's paper?"

The librarian nodded. "Yes. It was a beautiful tribute to a fine young man. How is your father?"

Em sighed and dried her eyes. "About the same; doesn't talk much, just sits and stares. He did go to his office yesterday and made some house calls. He had to; there's so much sickness in town this time of year. Doctor Freetag is put to it just taking care of his own practice, let alone Papa's."

"Well, don't worry. Maylen will come around. Getting involved with his patients will be good for him. He is not the only father who has lost a son in the war." The librarian picked up an envelope from her desk. "While you are out at the charging desk this morning, I'd like you to sort out these newspaper items I have clipped, and arrange them chronologically. They are all concerned with the war.

It may be some time before we'll have a book about it. In the meantime we can use these clippings to answer any questions that may be asked."

Em sat at a small table in the charging desk area and emptied the clippings from the envelope. She began reading, then sorted according to dates. Soon she had the events of the war spread out before her; the blowing up of the *Maine*, the declaration of war, the capture of the Spanish fleet in the Pacific by Admiral Dewey, the call for volunteers, the embarking of the troops at Tampa for Cuba, the arrival of the Rough Riders in Santiago Bay, the taking of San Juan Hill by the Rough Riders.

Em paused and read that last article again. That wasn't the way Ashton had described it. It was up Kettle Hill that Colonel Roosevelt, on horseback, had led his men. She would ask Ashton— She dropped the clipping. Oh, Ashton, Ashton! For a second she had forgotten! She took a handkerchief from her pocket, dried the sudden tears, and blew her nose. She would have to ask Charlie. He had been there too.

But when would she have a chance to talk with Charlie? Now that Ashton was gone, he wouldn't be calling at the house anymore, she supposed. She couldn't help wondering if he were calling on Molly Flannery. The bicycle club was having a New Year's Eve party next Saturday at Dottie's. Each girl was to invite a young man. But she, Em, wouldn't be there since she was in mourning. She and Mama were wearing black now, and would continue to do so for a year. Vic and Papa had black crepe bands sewn on the sleeves of their coats.

In all likelihood Molly would ask Charlie to the party. Em sighed, glanced at the little gold watch pinned on her black shirtwaist, then across at the library clock to see if the two agreed.

She looked back at the clippings before her. But for all this, dear Ashton would be alive, his whole promising life stretched out before him. What a waste! All those lives lost, so great a price to pay in order that, as one article stated, the United States might become a world power.

She read about the treaty signed on December 10, and how the United States had agreed to pay Spain twenty million dollars for the Philippine Islands. Now all that remained was for Congress to ratify the treaty. From what she had read, Em gathered that that would take some doing since the Democratic Party was against the acquisition of the Philippines.

The clippings arranged in chronological order, Em distributed them into smaller envelopes, marking each with the subjects and dates.

Jessie came on duty at noon. Em and Miss Buchanan walked home together over the hard-packed snow on Main Street, their overshoes making a cold, creaking sound at every step. The sun shone, but the wind was biting. The two held their muffs before their faces for protection from the icy blasts.

"This cold snap will probably affect our business today," Miss Buchanan said. "I have been checking up on the children who have used the children's room since we opened and I find scarcely any have come from Lincoln School."

"Well, that building is on the other side of town. It's a long walk and I doubt if any children in that neighborhood would have carfare."

"Oh, come, come, Emmy! That's not too long a walk with a good book waiting at the other end. I think after the first of the year, I'll just prance myself out there and talk to those young ones. They have so little they should take advantage of the free pleasure available in their library. If I can just make them understand that the building and everything in it is *theirs*."

At home Em hung her wraps on the hall tree and sat down to remove her rubbers. Glancing at the closed doors to the parlor, the pain returned to her throat. Would they ever be able to use that room again?

It was delightfully warm in the sitting room, the base-burner throwing out heat through its isinglass doors, the red coals giving cheer to the whole room.

Vic, curled up in a big chair, glanced from his book at his sister, standing with her back to the stove.

"Is it cold out?" he asked.

"Bitter. I feel frozen clear through." Em turned and held her hands near the stove. "What are you reading?"

"*The Nurnberg Stove*. You know, Em, the way this boy feels about their stove is kind of like the way I feel about our base-burner. Of course I wouldn't be able to crawl into our stove and hide like he did." Vic laughed. "They'd see me right through the isinglass."

"I must bring you *The Dog of Flanders* by the same author."

"You don't need to. I'm going to the library myself this afternoon. Em," Vic went on, "Papa still hasn't let me tell him I want to be a doctor. Everytime I start to talk to him, he tells me to be quiet."

Em walked to the window and looked out. "I tell you what," she said, "this afternoon you go to the office and ask him if he has something he wants done. You could dust, arrange the magazines, and get him to show you how to wash his instruments. That's the way Ashton started."

"He did?"

"Yes. And maybe while you're there you can tell him how you feel about being a doctor. There he is now," she said, watching her father drive by the window in his one-seated sleigh.

Mama came in from the kitchen. "Papa's here. Dinner will be on the table in a jiffy. Wash your hands, Vic."

The clock on the mantel struck half-past twelve. Since Em had started working, the Dudley dinner hour had been changed to accommodate her schedule.

"We are eating in the kitchen today, too cold in the dining room," Mama said. She pushed back the top on the base-burner and peered in. "Vic, right after dinner you bring in a bucket of hard coal for this stove." She pushed the stove top into place. "I declare I don't know where this morning has gone. Of course it took me awhile to thaw out the water hydrant. I wish Maylen would consider piping water into the kitchen," Mama murmured to herself as she left.

Vic followed Mama from the room. Em watched her father coming toward the back door, his fur cap pulled down over his ears, his bag carried in a mittened hand. There was a forlorn droop to his shoulders. She turned away and stood before the closed doors to the parlor. Again, just now, listening to Mama and Vic, she had forgotten Ashton for a second. It had almost seemed that he was away at medical school and that Papa might be going to read one of his wonderful letters to all of them at the table. Papa's dejected figure brought back all the misery of their loss. Slowly she made her way through the cold dining room to the warm kitchen.

Miss Buchanan had taken Em's night duty on Wednesday, so Em took the librarian's Saturday night schedule. It was December 31, New Year's Eve, and Em was to close the library at eight o'clock instead of the usual nine.

She sat on the high stool behind the desk. There was a

book in her lap, but she was not reading. The silence was broken only by the tick of the clock. She looked at its big white face. Fifteen minutes after seven! This time last week Ashton was still with them. Right at this time, he had been watching them trim the tree. He had teased Papa a bit about the three old battered decorations Papa always insisted on hanging in the most conspicuous spots.

"Don't run these down, son," Papa had said. "They're a lot older than you are. You should respect their years. I remember as a boy I—" and Papa had launched into his usual Christmas Eve reminiscing, telling stories of his boyhood, stories they had heard every Christmas Eve for years and years.

Em brushed her hand across her eyes. She must not cry here.

At half-past seven Mr. Stewart, the janitor, came in. Each night the library was open he came back to lock up. He approached the desk.

"Not much business, Miss Dudley?"

"No. I think we could have closed at six really. It is still so cold?"

"Well, the wind has died down. But I looked at the thermometer just before I left home and it was seven below." He went into the reading room, took the evening newspaper from a rack and sat down to read.

The clock ticked on. Em dropped a slip of paper in her book to mark her place and walked back into the stacks. It wasn't often that she had time to browse, deciding which books she wanted to read someday. She walked through the gate from the stacks to the table in the main lobby and looked at the new books Miss Buchanan kept there.

She wished she could get Papa to read something. This one—*David Harum*—looked amusing. She had read a review of it in *McClure's Magazine* that compared the author, Edward Westcott, to Mark Twain and Bret Harte, surely high recommendation.

The silence was broken by the opening of the front door. From where she stood at the table Em could look down through the glass to the lower lobby. Her heart gave a lunge, then settled down to a steady pounding. A man stomped snow from his feet, unbuttoned his overcoat, and pulled a toboggan cap from his head, revealing the thick blond hair of Charlie Hargrove!

Em's first thought was: he is not taking Molly Flannery to the bicycle club party!

Hastily she returned to the charging desk and sat on the high stool. How often she had imagined this scene before, and always she had been at the desk, the cool, competent, and dignified librarian. At last Charlie was to see her here. She took the book and opened it, keeping her eyes on the printed page, but not seeing a word.

"Ahem! Miss Librarian, is this what the taxpayers pay you for? Just to sit around and read!" He stood in front of her and smiled.

"Oh, hello, Charlie!" She closed her book. "Things are very quiet tonight, no business at all. I should think you would be going to a New Year's Eve party."

Charlie's smile disappeared. "I was invited to several, but somehow I couldn't bring myself to go. I telephoned your home to see if I could call on you. Your mother said you were here. May I see you home when the library closes? I want to talk about Ashton."

Em stood up and glanced at the clock; fifteen to eight. "Well, I told Papa I would go over to his office and walk home with him."

"Is there a telephone here? Could you call him? I really need to talk to you."

Em swallowed hard. "I guess I could."

He looked around. "Say this place is beautiful. I haven't been here since the opening night and then I was only upstairs."

How well I know, Em thought to herself. "Why don't you look around while I call Papa," she said.

In Miss Buchanan's office she gave Papa's office number to central. "Papa," she said when he answered, "I won't be coming to your office. Charlie Hargrove is going to see me home."

The doctor let out with a loud "Humph! That popinjay! What does *he* want?"

"To walk home with me." Oh dear, what if Papa said she couldn't. She was in the habit of obeying him; but after all she *was* eighteen, surely she had a right to— "Papa, Charlie passed up several invitations to New Year's Eve parties. He says he wants to talk to me about Ashton."

There was a silence at the other end of the line, then, "Oh, well, all right. I wouldn't know why you would want to walk with him, him and his bragging ways."

"Papa, Charlie does not brag. It's his father who does. Remember?"

"Well, see that he's gone by the time I get home. I can't bear the sight of him."

Returning the receiver to its hook, Em stood there a moment. She knew why Papa had this aversion to Charlie. The war had spared Charlie, but not Ashton and to Papa's mind Ashton's life had held so much more promise than did that of gay, lighthearted Charlie. But who knew what course Charlie's life might be taking, by the time he was twenty-five? Papa shouldn't hold his youth against him.

At eight o'clock Mr. Stewart turned out the lights in the reading room. Charlie waited down at the front door while Em put on her wraps. She glanced in the mirror as she tied the ribbons of her black velvet hood under her chin.

Her cheeks were rosy, as though she had already been out in the cold. Fastening her coat, she turned up the collar, then put on her gloves, picked up her muff, and descended the steps to the lower lobby.

Mr. Stewart called after her, "Good night, Miss Dudley."

"Good night, Mr. Stewart." She looked up at Charlie. And what a *good* night this was! Charlie had seen her in all the glory of her new position and heard her called *Miss* Dudley just as though she really was a librarian. Well, she *was*, wasn't she? She had worked in this lovely place for a whole month and this afternoon had been given her first check, a check reposing this very minute in her pocketbook, a check signed by Mr. Tiller, treasurer of the Library Board, a check for twenty dollars!

Charlie held the door open for her.

Outside, crispy, cold air touched her face. Snow hid the dingy spots in Harper City; but even without it, Em would have thought the night beautiful. Suddenly she remembered Ashton! How could she feel happy? This was the third time she had forgotten!

"You know, Em," Charlie began as they reached the sidewalk, "ever since Ashton's funeral last Tuesday, I have been doing an awful lot of thinking. Serious thinking," he added. "I've always been sort of harum-scarum, I guess, without much thought of the future. But somehow, now, I feel I've got to amount to something. Otherwise Ashton's saving my life will be meaningless. If he had lived he could have given so much to the world, and not just as a doctor. He was great, really great. That night we talked, right after we landed in Cuba, I found out what he was like. He could just bring out the best that was in a fellow. Do you know what I mean?"

Em clasped her hands tight inside her muff. "Oh, yes,

yes. Ashton was like that and even more." She launched into a description of Ashton's growing up, of what he had meant to her and to the rest of the family.

Charlie continued, "Well, I've made up my mind to really work now on my own life and make it worthy of Ashton. I'm going to start in at Indiana University on February first. I talked it over with Father and he is pleased with my decision."

Em's first thought was, Charlie would be leaving town! And just when he seemed to be noticing her! "Why, that's fine," she said, trying to make her voice sound enthusiastic.

"Right off I thought of you, Em. I wanted to ask if you thought Ashton would approve. Of course, I don't really know yet what line of work I want to follow, whether it will be law or something else. But Father says the important thing is to get started at laying the foundation for my education. Specialization can come later."

Recovering from her first reaction, Em said slowly, "I know Ashton would like you to go to the University. In his letter about meeting you, he said you had matured a great deal."

"He did? Well, from now on I'm going to try to live up to his opinion. And Em, I was wondering if you'd mind if I wrote to you sometimes while I'm away. I know myself pretty well, and I'm likely to stray from all these good resolutions I'm making right now. Maybe writing to you might help me remember Ashton and all that he stands for. And if you could write to me occasionally, it would sure help."

Em relaxed. "I'll be glad to write to you, Charlie. I won't have much to write about except what's happening at the library."

"Well, say, that will be great! Do you like working there?"

"Oh, yes. I learn something everyday. You never know what someone will ask next. And I love working with the children, talking to them, helping them find good books. And, once they get to know you, the things they do tell! Their mothers would die if they knew." Em gave a short laugh, took a little run and slid on a smooth piece of ice.

Charlie caught up with her. "I expect working in a library is almost like going to college; with all those books around you're bound to keep learning all the time."

"I try to. I'm following a special reading program now, trying to fill in the gaps in my education." Em took another slide. She felt she was getting to know Charlie better and better. This was even nicer than that walk under the umbrella.

All too soon the Dudley house appeared. They walked up to the steps and paused.

"Would you like to come in?" she asked. "I could make you some hot chocolate."

"I don't think I should tonight, Em, with your family in mourning. But later, before I leave for the University, I'd like to call, if I may."

"I'll be glad to see you anytime, Charlie."

"Do you always work Saturday nights at the library?"

"Not usually. My regular night is Wednesday."

"Maybe you wouldn't mind if I showed up around nine on Wednesdays and walked you home." He took off his toboggan cap and held out his hand. "Thanks for listening to me. Good night, Em, and happy New Year."

"Good night, Charlie. I know it will be a good New Year for you."

Even after she got inside the hall she could still feel the pressure of his fingers.

She stayed awake a long time that night, living over every minute, from the time she saw him enter the library until he had taken her hand at the steps. She was awake at twelve and heard the church bells ring, the factory whistles and fire whistle sounding in the New Year, 1899! What did it hold for her?

Ashton was gone. "Take two looks at everything, one for you and one for me," he had said.

"Oh, I will, Ashton," she whispered, "I will."

Chapter 15

"Thank You, Miss Dudley"

New Year's Day, Em attended church with her father. The minister called his sermon "The Last Year," and by that he meant that the year ahead, 1899, was the last of the nineteenth century. And, he asked his congregation, what were they doing to prepare themselves for the twentieth century looming so closely before them?

It was a sobering thought, Em decided to herself. There didn't seem to be anything spectacular she could do, except try to do a good job at the library. Now Charlie, deciding to go to the University right away, was a fellow who would really be working on a worthwhile future when the new century rolled in.

She wondered what kind of letters he would write her. Or if, indeed, he would write her at all. She must not fool herself about Charlie. He just might forget all those high-sounding ideas he had spoken of last night. At present Ashton's death seemed to have affected him greatly. But would he still be influenced by his memory three months from now? Charlie was an only child; perhaps his parents *had* indulged him too much for his own good. There were those in town who said the judge and his wife had spoiled their son. But Em didn't agree. Charlie was a little self-centered and impulsive to be sure, but he was sensitive and capable of deep feeling, otherwise Ashton's death would not have left its mark on him.

Walking to church this morning, Papa had said little. She glanced at him now. His eyes were closed. Was he listening to the sermon? Probably not. More than likely it was thoughts of Ashton that filled his mind. Papa should be throwing off his depression by this time, or at least trying to. What could she say to him that would bring back the tart-tongued, straight-forward, no-nonsense Doc Dudley the whole town knew and respected? She was sure Mama was worried about him too.

After the benediction the doctor hurried up the aisle and out the front door, not waiting for the usual handshaking that always took place in the back of the church at the end of a service. Em talked to several who greeted her and sympathetically mentioned her recent loss. At the door the minister took her hand.

"I wanted to speak to your father, Emeline. How is he?"

Em hesitated, then blurted out, "He is bitter and angry, I'm afraid. I wish you would speak to him. It is hard for us to reach him."

"Sorry to hear that. I'll try to call on him this week."

Outside, Em could see her father striding along toward home, his fur cap pulled down, his shoulders hunched, his hands in his overcoat pockets. She ran to catch up.

"Papa, wait," she called.

The doctor turned around, then stood on the corner until she caught up.

"Reverend Roxberry was disappointed that you didn't speak to him." Em fell in step beside him.

"Had to get out of there," the doctor growled. "I was in no mood to listen to his mealy-mouthed platitudes."

"Papa! You know very well he isn't like that. He genuinely wants to help you."

"Can he bring Ashton back? Can he wipe out that war? The war that took my son? Let him save his syrupy words for someone else. Nothing can blot out the fact that my son is gone!"

"But Papa, you have another son. Did Vic tell you anything yesterday at the office?"

"Vic? He did come bothering around at the office, said he wanted to help me. But I sent him home. Couldn't be pestered by having him around."

"Oh, Papa, you didn't!" Em exclaimed. She straightened her shoulders angrily and jabbed her hands in her muff. "Dr. Maylen Dudley, I think you are horrid! And if Ashton were here he would say the same. Do you know what you are doing to Vic? You are making him feel that he counts for nothing. He had something very important to tell you."

The doctor looked at Em, shaken by her angry vehemence. "Tut, tut, there, young lady, that's no way to speak to your father! I'll have none of that! If having a job and making your own money are making you impudent you will just have to quit. You may be eighteen, but I'm still your father!" he blustered.

"I'll never forget that you are. But I know too that Vic is my brother and he deserves to be loved and respected by you. Ashton loved Vic. Remember how Ashton and I went all over the neighborhood saying that we had a new baby brother? Ashton was so proud of him."

The doctor simmered down and said softly, "I remember, Em."

"What Vic's been trying to tell you, Papa, is that he wants to be a doctor and would like to help in your office so he can learn from you. Please don't discourage him. He may not actually turn out to be a doctor, but right now he is very sincere. And with Ashton's example before him, who knows, he might really make it."

They walked along in silence. Em's blood pressure returned to normal. Had she gotten through to him? Imagine her, speaking to Papa in anger. But he needed a jolt. Vic had been very subdued at breakfast. Maybe his inflamed eyes did not indicate a cold as Mama had thought. He might have been crying.

All through the noon meal the doctor said little. Em did most of the talking, giving Mama an account of the sermon. Vic ate in silence, now and then surreptitiously holding a morsel of food under the table for Teddy's waiting mouth. This was a habit frowned on by Papa. But today Papa chose to ignore it, although Em was sure he knew what was going on. Several times she caught him looking thoughtfully at Vic.

The pudding eaten, second cups of coffee poured, Dr. Dudley said to Vic, "Victor, I'm hitching Prince to the sleigh to make a call in the country. Think your cold is well enough for you to come along?"

Em was sure she would never forget the expression of joy on her brother's face. She *had* reached her father! Anger, properly channeled, could be a good thing at times, she thought, as Mama beamed at Papa and Vic.

In January, circulation figures at the Harper City Public Library began to soar. With Christmas and its time-consuming festivities behind them, the town's citizens began to discover the pleasures Mr. Carnegie's gift could provide.

Miss Buchanan not only visited Lincoln School but also "pranced" herself to the others, with a special invitation for the children to "join" the library; the result, a crowded children's room each day after school.

Em and Jessie took turns keeping order and quiet there.

Em, however, was better at it than Jessie. Miss Buchanan soon discovered Em's aptitude at discipline.

"Emeline, I believe I'll just assign the children's room to you permanently. You do have a way about you that keeps the children quiet and well behaved." The librarian laughed. "You must have inherited your father's forcefulness or the glint in his eye that commands respect and obedience. Anyway you seem to be able to make them toe the mark."

Em laughed. "Oh, Miss Buchanan, you make me sound like an ogre."

"Not at all. Children like discipline, that is, friendly discipline. In dealing with children one should respect their ideas as much as those of adults. And, heavens to Betsy, the things you can learn in dealing with the younger generation, once you have gained their confidence."

With this new assignment, Em began reading the juvenile books that had been published since her own childhood. If she was to be able to suggest books, she must know her wares. Her adult reading list was supplanted by the latest works of Eliza Orne White, Laura Richards, Everett Tomlinson and Kate Douglas Wiggin.

Charlie did not forget that she was on duty Wednesday nights. He turned up punctually at a quarter to nine on those evenings. Wednesday grew to be Em's favorite day. Sometimes looking in the mirror, before she went to the library at noon, she wished she didn't look so somber. Black did nothing for her at all. In fact, it made her complexion look downright sallow. It was Mama who suggested that Em wear a bit of white lace around the top of her high collar.

"And," Mama went on, "wear my cameo brooch at your throat."

"Don't you think it might be too much with my watch?"

Em asked. "I don't want to be gaudy, especially not when I am in mourning."

"It won't be too much. And since Miss Buchanan has put you in charge of the children's room, you must think of the young people you are going to serve. I remember when I was a child I loved teachers who wore pretty clothes and was depressed by those who wore dowdy ones. Maybe you should stop wearing mourning altogether in two or three months."

"Oh, no, Mama, I must wear it at least for a year for Ashton."

"I'm not sure Ashton would want you to. He was a great one for children. He'd probably tell you to dress up and be gay for the young ones." Mama returned to her knitting. "When will Charlie leave for college?"

"Next Sunday."

"Then this will be the last Wednesday he'll see you home. Why don't you ask him in tonight? Fix him some hot chocolate. And I'm baking a cake this afternoon."

"Well, Mama, you know how Papa feels about Charlie. I'm afraid if he came in and found Charlie here, well, you know Papa. There's no telling what he might say."

Mama sighed. "Yes, Maylen does resent Charlie, resents him because he is alive and Ashton isn't. Well, suit yourself. But if it were I, I would ask Charlie in tonight."

Em thought of Mama's advice after she reached the library. It would be nice to be with Charlie a little while longer tonight, but what if Papa came in and said something embarrassing?

When the after-school rush began in the children's room, Em went in to keep order and help with book selection.

A boy approached her. "Say, aren't you the doctor's daughter?"

Em looked down into a face that seemed familiar. "Yes, I am."

"Well say, don't you remember me? I'm Billy Sessions. Your papa sewed my head." He smiled broadly.

"Why, of course. You're the boy who never let out a peep while he was doing it, either." Em looked at his forehead. "It left a little scar, I see."

"Yep, and I'm glad, too, because when I show it to the kids they really believe I had stitches. Say, are you the library lady in here?"

"Yes. May I help you?"

"I've got my slip here all signed for a card. Can I get a book today?" He pulled a white card from his pocket.

"Yes. What have you read that you liked?"

"When we lived in Chicago I read the Henty books and lots by Alger. I got *Treasure Island* for Christmas and I guess I must have read it about four times already."

"You sound as though you are a good reader, Billy. I read a book recently that I imagine you will like. Let's see if it is in." Em led the way to the shelves. "You're in luck; it's here." She handed him *The Aztec Treasure House.*

Billy turned through the pages. "What's it about?"

"Well, there's an exciting search for treasure; there's mystery and, as you read, the characters become real live people to you. It almost seems that you are there yourself. And there is a little donkey in it you'll never forget. If you want something exciting, this book is the one."

"Gee, it sounds almost as good as *Treasure Island.* I'll take it."

"All right. You go out to the desk in the adult room. They will make you a borrower's card and stamp your book. Be very quiet. Walk softly and, mind, no loud talking." Em walked him toward the door.

"Thank you, Miss—"

"Dudley."

"Thank you, Miss Dudley."

"You are welcome, Billy."

She walked to the windows and looked out on Main Street. Warmer temperatures had brought a thaw; the sidewalk and street were thick with gray slush. Now Billy would go home, she thought, and, curled up with his book, he could travel miles away to the lost city of the Aztecs and forget the drab, sloppy streets of Harper City. What a good thing she had read that book. When Billy returned it they could talk about it and be friends because of the book they had shared.

She looked at the children, seated at the tables, standing at the shelves. She wished she knew their names. Knowing Billy's had put them on a friendly basis. If Miss Buchanan let her continue in here, perhaps in time she would get to know more of the children by name and they would learn hers.

Em went home to supper at five, returning at six. Hanging up her wraps at the library, she looked at herself in the mirror. Yes, Mama's brooch and the bit of lace did improve her appearance. Would Charlie notice? What if he didn't come? What if some girl who was not in mourning and could go to parties should attract his attention? Last week he had asked to take her to the Opera House where a stock company was performing. She had explained that when one was in mourning one did not go to parties or to places of entertainment. Charlie had apologized for asking, saying he should have remembered. But what if some other girl—!

She went out to the charging desk.

"How's the weather outside?" Miss Buchanan asked.

"Not quite so sloppy. It's colder and the slush is freezing up. Rather difficult walking." She watched Jessie and the librarian leave, then looked at the clock. Six, seven, eight, nine—three hours until she would see Charlie coming up the steps of the outer lobby. *Would* see? She better make that *might* see.

Fortunately it was a busy night for Em. She didn't even have time to look into a juvenile book she had brought to the desk to read. Mr. Kipling's *Captains Courageous* would have to be read at another time.

Em had discovered that she had a good knowledge of girls' books but was not as sure of herself when it came to books for boys. Just knowing that Vic or Ashton had liked a certain book was not enough. She actually had to know what the book was about. She had to read them. Already she had learned that with children one must never pretend to know something one did not. A child could see through pretense quick as a wink.

The library was full of activity. There were many people at the tables in the reading room, and others crowded around the desk, returning books, checking out new selections. Patrons browsed in the stacks. Em was flushed and a little excited at having the library revolve about her. The building was fulfilling the function for which it had been created. Em knew she wasn't keeping the place as quiet as Miss Buchanan liked to have it, but she didn't have time tonight to go around shushing people.

Most of the borrowers had left by twenty minutes to nine. Mr. Stewart came in and went to the reading room to straighten up. Em got the desk in order, then glanced at the clock. Ten minutes to nine. He wasn't coming! Other Wednesday nights he had been here by a quarter to nine.

Well, that was that. She had seen the last of Charlie. Next Sunday he would leave for college, without seeing her. She was sure of it as the clock ticked on.

She went to the back room to wash her hands. When

she returned Charlie stood on the other side of the counter.

"Fine thing! No librarian on the job. What kind of service are the taxpayers getting for their money?" he exclaimed with a teasing grin.

"Sorry, sir," Em said with feigned meekness. "It won't happen again, sir. What can I do for you, sir?"

"Let me walk you home, ma'am."

"With pleasure, sir."

Charlie laughed and turned to look at the clock. The lights in the reading room went off. "All right, Miss Dudley, let's go."

It was a beautiful walk home! The slippery sidewalks made it necessary for Em to cling to Charlie's arm for support. No one would have guessed that this same young librarian, a few hours before, had made the journey to the library totally unassisted.

"It seems as though the distance between the library and your house gets shorter every time, Em," he said looking up at the Dudleys' home.

"Why don't you come in and have something to eat?" Em suggested.

"It's not too late?"

"No. Come on."

Inside there was a lighted lamp in the hall, one in the sitting room and one in the kitchen. This, Em knew, was Mama's doing. She and Vic must have gone to bed. But what about Papa? Had he come home from the office and gone to bed too?

In the kitchen Charlie sat at the table while Em tied on an apron, put a piece of wood in the range, and prepared the chocolate. She brought the cake from the pantry.

"You look very domestic in that apron, Em. Can you cook?"

"Fairly well, I guess you could say. With practice I might

be good at it. Mama loves to cook, so I don't get much chance around here." Em cut the cake.

Sitting at the table, sipping the hot drink and eating Mama's delicious cake, Em knew she had never been so happy. Charlie ate his cake with good appetite and had a second piece. Em noted how his blond hair glistened in the lamplight. She couldn't understand why so good-looking a man should want to call on her.

Charlie glanced at the large calendar on the wall. "You know what, Em? It was just a month ago that Ashton died. Seems longer, doesn't it. I almost forgot."

Em gave a start. In her happiness she too had forgotten. She looked at the calendar, January 25. "It's queer, the way life goes on," she said slowly. "When someones dies, you think you just can't live without him, but you do, and you keep thinking of him less frequently all the time. I wish we could do something to keep Ashton's memory alive."

"Have some kind of memorial?"

"Yes. I've thought about it before, but haven't come up with anything in particular," Em said. She heard the front door close. Papa!

"I'll put my mind to it too," Charlie said.

"What the devil!" Dr. Dudley stood in the doorway glowering at Charlie.

Charlie rose. "Good evening, Doctor Dudley. Em is feeding me. This is mighty good cake."

The doctor said nothing.

"Papa," Em said, with a plea for understanding in her tone, "Charlie is leaving for college on Sunday."

"Oh, is he now!" The doctor pulled out his watch. "And it is high time he was leaving for home right now. It's after ten o'clock."

"Papa!" Em had never known him to be so rude. Why was he doing this to her?

"Yes, sir, I was just going." Charlie got up, slipped his chair under the table and went into the hall for his coat.

Em gave her father a hurt look and followed. "Oh, Charlie, I'm sorry Papa—"

"Don't worry about it, Em. I understand. It's Ashton, isn't it?"

Em nodded. "He just can't forget for a minute."

Charlie stood at the door and held out his hand. "Good-bye, Em. I'll write and tell you about things. Take care of yourself. I hope you enjoy your work in the library."

He was gone!

In bed she cried. Ashton was dead and now Charlie had left. Without Charlie the future at this moment seemed drab. There would be no magic to Wednesday nights. She dried her eyes and put her handkerchief under the pillow. Still, there were those after-school rushes when she would be holding forth in the children's room.

"Thank you, Miss Dudley!" That had been nice to hear. In time she would know many children. She would become their "library lady." With Charlie gone, she would concentrate on her job and become the best "library lady" in Indiana! Ashton would like that.

"Thank you, Miss Dudley!"

She was asleep.

Chapter 16

The Right-Size Book

February brought a false spring; the snow melted leaving the ground muddy and soft. Some days the air was almost balmy.

Returning from the library each day, Em looked expectantly at the hall table for the anticipated letter. Not seeing it there, she hopefully continued to the dining room, half expecting to see an envelope at her place.

At the library she was too busy to give more than an occasional thought to Charlie, but at home she thought of him often. That business of an exchange of letters between them had been just so much idle talk, she decided. He was not going to write to her. And of course she couldn't write to him first.

During many sleepless periods at night she thought of how it might have been if Charlie had discovered her when they were still in high school. She pictured them walking together through the halls, and then, school dismissed, she could see him walking home with her, and perhaps carrying her books. If that had happened he might have written to her during the war and now, away at college, he might have continued the correspondence.

There were no two ways about it, she had come into his life too late. He knew so many girls in Harper City and now there must be lots of pretty ones at college. She must face it, he was not going to write to her.

Then, on March 1, a Wednesday, as she opened the front door on her way to the library, Mr. Wallace was mounting the steps with a letter in his hand.

"This one is for you, Emmy Lou," he said as he handed it to her.

"Thank you, Mr. Wallace."

The postman gone, she stood there looking at her name scrawled across the envelope. This must be Charlie's writing; the postmark was Bloomington. There wasn't time to go back into the house to read it. She stuck the letter inside her muff and held onto the envelope with both hands as she went down the steps.

How fitting that it should come on a Wednesday. She clasped the letter tighter and walked faster.

At the library, her coat removed, she stuck the letter into the deep pocket of her black skirt. Sitting at the charging desk, she watched Miss Buchanan and Jessie leave. Only the clock's tick broke the silence. Seldom were there any patrons this time of day.

Em took the letter out and slit the envelope with a hairpin and read:

Dear Em,

I can imagine that you have given up on me, promising to write as I did, and then not doing it.

Well, it's this way. The past month has been terrible, just terrible! As you know, good old Harper City High School gave me a diploma even though I didn't finish the last semester. And then I went off to war and forgot there were such things as study and books.

What a rude awakening when I arrived here. Those first weeks, I tried to study, and my mind would wander. I'd think about the war and Colonel Roosevelt, about those horrible steamy days in Cuba. I thought of Ashton and what his death has done to your father. I thought of the way I wasted time in my father's office last fall, pretending to read law, but not concentrating enough for any of it to stick, and more often than not, I'd think of a pretty librarian.

The way things were going I knew I would be thrown out on my ear by spring vacation if I didn't learn how to concentrate. Tad Wilson is a senior, a very bright student. He is giving me two tutoring sessions a week. Now I think maybe I'm going to make it.

When the going gets tough, thinking of Ashton gives me a boost. My acquaintance with him was short, but I'll never forget him.

Do write, Em, and tell me about yourself, your family and the library. Believe me, I'm a fellow who needs encouragement.

Sincerely yours,
Charlie Hargrove

She read it again. She wished Papa didn't resent Charlie. At home she was careful not to mention his name in front of Papa. Should she tell him about this letter? No, she better not. It was difficult not being able to talk to Papa about Charlie.

"Ahem! Pardon me."

Em looked up from the letter into the stern face of a young man whose mustache spread across his upper lip like a two-pointed saber. Hastily she replaced the letter in its envelope.

"May I help you?"

"I'm Jim Addison of the *News*. Do you have any books about the recent war in Cuba?"

"We have two, but they are out in circulation, were borrowed yesterday, as a matter of fact. But we do have several recent magazine articles listed." She went to a desk and took a card from the drawer. Handing it to the

reporter she said, "These are the titles. If you will tell me
which you would like to see, I'll get them from our files.
We also have a collection of newspaper clippings, but I
presume you have access to back numbers of the *News*."

"Yes, I do." He took the card.

Em eyed him as he read. She wondered what he'd look
like if he smiled, and if he had been in the war. He
seemed older than Charlie, but maybe it was the mustache
that added years.

"I'd like to see the articles in *Scribner's*, *Harpers* and
McClure's that you have listed here, if I may."

"Certainly." She took the card again. "I'll get them for
you." She went to the back room where past issues of magazines were kept in alphabetical order on special shelves.
She returned with the three he had asked for. "Here they
are." He handed her his library card. "Oh, I'm sorry, Mr.
Addison, but magazines cannot be taken from the building.
You'll have to use them here."

"I borrowed magazines from the Indianapolis library
when I lived there," the man protested. "You see, I'm a
writer, a reporter on an assignment. I *must* take these
home."

Em's temper flared as she looked him straight in the
eyes. "It is against our rules. You will have to use them
here." Miss Buchanan had warned Jessie and Em that there
would be patrons like this one. "Be firm and stand your
ground," the librarian had said. "Don't break the rules for
anyone no matter what or who the person is. Be polite,
of course, at all times."

"I'm afraid you don't understand, Miss—ah—what *is* your
name?"

"Dudley."

He frowned. "You don't understand, Miss Dudley. I have
to write a feature article for a special edition of the *News*

to come out in April, on the first anniversary of our declaration of war against Spain. I can't write the article here."

"I'm afraid you'll have to or else do it without these magazines!" Em snapped. She pulled herself up short. Watch out, Miss Dudley! "Why don't you take them into the reading room and work at one of the tables?" she asked in a more moderate tone.

Jim Addison gave her a long hard look; seeing that she had no intention of backing down, he sighed and picked up the magazines. "Oh, very well, I'll use them here."

Em watched him go through the big arched doorway into the reading room. He put his overcoat and hat on another chair, then sat down and began to turn through the magazines. Soon his head was bent over the notebook in which he wrote.

Em's anger at the man's demand for special privilege subsided and she felt a little thrill of triumph. Miss Buchanan had said the rules had been made with the good of the greatest number of people in mind. Now those magazines would be on the premises for others who might want to use them today. But she had very nearly lost her temper completely. For a minute there she must have sounded like Papa at his pepperiest.

She rescued her precious letter from the floor where it had dropped. After reading it again, she carefully put it into her pocket. Her eyes chanced on the arch to the reading room. The young reporter was watching her. Hastily he bent again over his notebook and wrote industriously.

At one o'clock Jessie and Miss Buchanan returned. Jessie took over at the charging desk. Em went into the librarian's office to learn her afternoon assignment.

"Emmy Lou, that book came this morning. I think I mentioned it to you before." Miss Buchanan picked up a book from her desk. "It is *Books for the Young,* a list of good reading for children. It was compiled by a librarian in Hartford, Connecticut. Besides the lists of books which she has selected very carefully, Miss Hewins has written an outstanding preface. I think you will have time to look it over before the school rush. Eventually I want you to list the books she recommends that we do not have and we'll purchase them as we have the funds. I want you and me to build a good basic collection for our children's room."

Em took the book into the children's room and sat at one of the low tables to read. "Give children something they are growing up to and not away from," she read. What a good statement. That probably meant, make them stretch a little in their reading.

She recalled how she had liked to read "hard" books in which she had to skip unknown words; and how the meaning of the difficult words frequently came to her from the content of the sentence, and, after asking Ashton the pronunciation, she would use the new words to impress her schoolmates.

Once, before Vic was born, Mama had taken Em to Iseley's book department and let her buy a book of her own choice.

"Choose carefully, Emmy Lou," she had said. "It's as important for a book to be the right size for your mind as it is for a hat to be the right size for your head. Get either too small and it will pinch like the dickens. Don't try to squeeze your mind into a 'small book'; one that's too big isn't comfortable either."

Em looked about the children's room. All these wonderful books, and her job was to see that each child got a book that was the right size for him. It was a tall order. She didn't know much about it yet, but she could learn, and *would* too!

Someone entered the room. Em looked up. It was the reporter, and he smiled at her.

"I just wanted to tell you, Miss Dudley, that I returned the magazines to the desk. Thank you very much. I may have to come back and do some more work. I'd like very much to see those two books you spoke of. When do you think they will be returned?"

"That's hard to say. As I told you they were just borrowed yesterday. Is there any way I could telephone you when they come back?" She should make up to him for that sudden loss of temper.

"I don't have a telephone at home but we do at the newspaper office. I'll write the number for you." He wrote on a scrap of paper and handed it to her. "I'll be ever so much obliged to you."

"It's too bad you have to write the article right away. I noticed in *Publisher's Weekly* that a new book is coming out in the summer by Theodore Roosevelt to be called *The Rough Riders*. He was the leader of that group, you know."

"Yes, indeed, I do know. I had an uncle from Wyoming who was with the Rough Riders. I'll probably want to buy the book for myself."

"I'm sure it will be very popular. I have a friend who was with the Rough Riders," Em added on impulse.

"Well, then you know what a great outfit it was. Who is he? I might know him." The reporter looked down at her interestedly.

"Charlie Hargrove."

"Oh, sure, the judge's son. He isn't in town now, is he?"

"No, he's going to the University."

"I didn't think he was around. He was going with a cousin of mine for a while, Molly Flannery. Do you know her?"

Em looked down at her book. Know her! Well, did she ever! "Yes, I know Molly. We graduated in the same class and now we belong to the same bicycle club. But since I'm working here, I don't see her often. I can't get to the meetings."

"Say," he looked at her more closely, "aren't you Doc Dudley's daughter?"

"Yes."

"Then you are Ashton Dudley's sister." Em nodded. "Molly told me about him. You know, it just came to me. I might do my article on a more personal basis by bringing in the war records of your brother and Charlie Hargrove." He thought a moment. "Yes-sir-ee! I just might do that!"

At four o'clock that same day, the children flocked into the room and quickly filled the small chairs. Some bent over picture books, others read books and magazines. They stood at the shelves hunting the just-right book to take home. Em walked about keeping things as quiet as possible and giving help where it was needed.

It was really noisier in the adult room, as children crowded around the charging desk to have their books checked out. At the height of the rush Em saw Miss Buchanan and the president of the Library Board, Mr. Long, standing at the doorway looking things over.

She wondered what they were talking about. Was she doing something wrong? She was sure she was not. She looked the other way, turning back to the shelves and selecting the *Merry Adventures of Robin Hood* for a boy. She watched him sit down with the book, knowing that once the boy had seen Howard Pyle's illustrations he would be completely "sold."

Em went home to supper at five, returning at six. When Miss Buchanan was ready to leave she came out to the charging desk and spoke to Em.

"I presume you saw that Bert Long was in this afternoon." Em nodded. "Well, I wanted him to see for himself what happens here when school is out. Something just has to be done about all that bedlam around the charging desk. Bert agrees. So we are ordering a charging desk for the children's room. That way you can charge their books and keep the children in there until they are ready to leave. With the doors closed we can keep things fairly quiet out here. Furthermore, I think we are going to add another person to the staff in April."

"That's good," Em said. "Do you have any idea who it will be?"

"No. We have letters from several applicants. I haven't made up my mind which one will work out best. At the meeting last night the Board voted that we open the reading room to the public on Sunday afternoons from two until six, beginning in April. Of course we won't lend any books, but one of us will have to be on duty every Sunday. So, if we get another staff member, our Sunday duty will come only every fourth week. I don't want to overwork you girls."

"You don't, Miss Buchanan. I love working in the children's room. I just wish I knew more so I'd be of more use to them. That book by Miss Hewins is very good. It's going to be a big help to me, I think."

Miss Buchanan pulled on a glove. "You are doing fine in there, Emmy Lou. Some morning let's sit down together and do some planning for the children's work. You be thinking about it."

When Em left the building at nine, she found Papa outside waiting for her.

"My last patient was out by a quarter to nine, so I thought I'd come over and save you walking to the office," he said as they set off on Main Street. "Did you have a good day?"

"Oh, yes." Em wished she could tell him about her letter from Charlie. "There was an interesting man in this afternoon. He's a reporter on the *News*. His name is Jim Addison."

Em described the trouble she had had over the magazines and the article the reporter was planning.

"I don't see why they want to rehash that war business. We had a bellyful of that last year. It's best forgotten. If one can, that is."

"Yes, Papa." Perhaps she shouldn't have told him about Jim Addison. She changed the subject. "How is Vic doing, Papa? Does he still come to your office after school?"

"Emmy, that boy is a fine little lad, and he really has become a help to me down there. There's a lot of Ashton in him."

"And a lot of Doc Dudley," Em added, squeezing his arm.

That night Emeline Dudley went to sleep with a letter under her pillow.

Chapter 17

"Remember the *Maine* and Ashton Dudley"

April brought several important events into Em's life: the new charging desk in the children's room, Jim Addison's article in the *News,* Sunday afternoon duty in the library, Charlie home for spring vacation, and the advent of a newcomer on the library staff. News of the latter was startling and unwelcome to Em's ears. At the March meeting of the Library Board, Molly Flannery was appointed to a place on the library staff!

"Molly's a bright little thing and has a good literary background," Miss Buchanan told Em and Jessie the morning after the board meeting. "I think she will work out well. When she comes, Em, you will be relieved of some of the adult assignments you have been carrying and can then devote more time to the children's work. Even those board members who were against having a children's room in this building, have come around. Those juvenile circulation figures don't lie. I couldn't be more satisfied with the way that room and its book collection are being used."

Molly came to work on April 1, looking lovely and attractive in a dark green skirt and light green shirtwaist. "You look like a real breath of spring," Jessie told her.

"You do indeed," Em added. Going into the children's

room to shelve the books that had been returned the day before, she thought that her own shirtwaist and skirt seemed even blacker than when she had put them on this morning.

She had received two more letters from Charlie and had answered both. He was coming home for spring vacation the last week in April. She *had* been excited about that, but now, with Molly here, looking as beautiful as a blooming lilac bush on a spring morning, and herself as drab and bleak as a cornfield in winter, well, what chance would she have with the gay, fun-loving Charlie?

That evening after supper she sat down in the living room with two new juvenile books in her lap.

"Well, what is our 'library lady' reading tonight?" Mama asked, picking up the darning basket from a low table beside her chair.

Em opened a book. "This is a story for girls by Laura Richards called *Margaret Montfort*. It's another in a series, the first was titled *The Three Margarets*." Em held up the other one. "And this one is for boys, *The Minute Boys of Lexington* by Edward Stratemeyer. I'm trying to keep up on the new books as they come in."

"Wasn't there another series by Laura Richards that you read when you were a child?" Mama asked.

"Um-huh. The *Queen Hildegarde* series and how I loved them."

Mama nodded. "You used to read lying flat on your stomach right there on the rug in front of the base-burner and Ashton would be over there in the window seat, his nose in a book too. Whenever I called, neither of you would hear. Such bookworms!"

Em opened a book to page one and read the first paragraph three times. Her mind kept wandering to Molly, her dark hair, her lovely eyes with the incredibly long lashes, and a complexion—oh, what a lovely complexion!

She felt her mother's eyes upon her. "What is it, Mama?"

"I think it is time you stopped wearing black shirtwaists. I made a surprise for you today, it's on my bed. Get it and see what you think of it."

Em went into the bedroom and returned with a white shirtwaist made of eyelet embroidery. "It's beautiful, Mama!"

"I kind of thought you'd like it. Wear it to church tomorrow so I can see it on you. I got out your other white waists and pressed out a few wrinkles. Now, no more black ones from now on. You owe it to your children to dress up a little. I'm sure Ashton would agree."

"Yes, I expect he would. He wanted me to be a good librarian."

"Before you sit down, get your straw sailor for me and I'll put a new ribbon band on it. I want you to put away the black winter hat."

On Monday Em started to the library feeling springy and pert. The collar of the new shirtwaist, held tight and high with stays, gave her confidence and dignity. Under one arm she carried the two juvenile books, under the other, an umbrella to protect her straw sailor from the rain that threatened.

Em's first Sunday duty came on April 23. She had carried the library key home with her on Saturday, and on Sunday afternoon at ten minutes to two she unlocked the heavy front door. Picking up the Sunday newspapers that lay outside, she entered.

Mounting the steps inside, she felt a thrill of power spread over her. She, Em Dudley, was in charge here! It was a big responsibility with which the taxpayers of Harper City had entrusted her.

Hanging her coat in Miss Buchanan's office, she picked up the newspapers and went out to the charging desk. She got out the small file box of newpaper cards and checked each one to show that the papers had been delivered for April 23. Then she took the papers to the reading room. She locked the doors to the stacks and bolted the two wooden gates on either side of the charging desk. No one was permitted in the stacks on Sunday.

The front door opened and an elderly gentleman went into the reading room. Mr. Earl was a daily visitor and was as familiar to the staff as the reading room furniture.

Em picked up the book cards from Saturday's circulation and began arranging the fiction alphabetically by author and the nonfiction by call numbers. With this filing done on Sunday, Monday mornings could be devoted to the "reading" of the shelves, that is, seeing that every book was in its proper place. "A book out of place is a book lost," Miss Buchanan had told her staff.

By three o'clock there were several in the reading room. Em finished filing the book cards, counting and recording the number for the circulation report. She wrote record cards for new borrowers and filed them. Desk chores finished, she went into the children's room for a book.

Returning, she sat at the back of the desk area and opened *The Peterkin Papers*. Usually she read only the new juvenile books, but today she would indulge herself. Ashton had read her this book when she was eight and what fun it had been laughing over the foolish doings of the Peterkin family. Some of the episodes Ashton had read to the whole family, and for a long time, whenever a problem came up, she or Ashton would say, "Papa, why don't we go ask the Lady from Philadelphia what to do, as the Peterkins did?"

Em turned the pages, looking at the illustrations. Tears dimmed her eyes as each one brought memories of Ashton.

"Good afternoon, Miss Dudley."

Em looked up. "Oh, Mr. Addison, hello." She rose and walked to the front counter.

"I hoped you would be on duty today," he said, putting his hat on the counter. "I wanted to tell you that my article will be in Tuesday's paper, April twenty-fifth. It was just a year ago on that day that Congress voted to declare war."

"I'll watch for it," she said.

"Well, I couldn't have written it without your help."

"That's the purpose of the library, to find material on any subject for which we are asked," Em answered a bit pompously. She was glad she had worn her new shirtwaist.

"I believe you will be surprised when you read it, and, I hope, pleased. I don't think it was exactly what Mr. Rhorer had in mind when he asked me to write it, but anyway he is publishing it as I wrote it. I think he had thought of a more flag-waving piece. But I like to do more realistic writing, without any glossing over of the real facts."

"Another Stephen Crane?" Em asked.

Jim Addison's eyebrows went up. "So, you know his work, do you? I wouldn't have thought many women read his stuff."

"Librarians read everything." She wondered if that didn't sound braggy. Relaxing a little, she told him of Ashton's contact with the author in Cuba.

The two were in such deep conversation that neither noticed a person standing at the other end of the counter. Only when he approached did Em turn around.

"Charlie! When did you come in?"

He gave a quick smile, then glanced at the reporter. "Been here quite awhile, but you two didn't hear me."

"Charlie, this is Mr. Addison, a reporter on the *News*. Mr. Addison, this is Mr. Hargrove."

"Charlie Hargrove? *The* Charlie Hargrove?" the reporter asked, extending his hand.

"The only one in these parts." Charlie shook his hand.

"Well, I'm glad to meet you in the flesh. Your father has told me a lot about you."

"Heavenly days! Has the judge been telling again about how I won the war singlehanded?"

Jim Addison grinned. "He did tell me a few tales about Cuba." He turned to Em. "You know, Miss Dudley, I believe Mr. Hargrove will be as interested in that April twenty-fifth issue of the *News* as you will be."

Em explained to Charlie about the article.

"Miss Dudley was so kind, looking up magazine articles and books for me," Jim Addison said, sending a big smile in Em's direction.

Charlie looked at the reporter, taking in his black hair, neatly parted in the middle and curling a bit on his forehead, his waxed mustache, his black overcoat and highly polished shoes. Charlie turned back to Em.

"I'm sorry. I must have interrupted your conversation. I'll step along into the reading room and glance over the papers." He was gone before Em could say a word.

"I must go too," Jim Addison said, picking up his hat. "Glad I got to meet Mr. Hargrove. Wish I could have known your brother. I think he was my kind of man."

Both men gone, Em sat down and picked up her book. She opened it. Somehow, at this moment, even the Peterkins didn't seem funny.

What was the matter with Charlie? Would he come back to the desk before he left? She glanced at the clock. Ten after five.

At five-thirty Mr. Stewart came. "Had many people in, Miss Dudley?" the janitor asked.

"The reading room was full in the middle of the afternoon. Most have gone now, however." Em stood at the counter and looked into the reading room. She could not see Charlie. Mr. Stewart went to the basement to take care of the furnace.

Em left the desk, unbolted a gate and crossed the lobby to the reading room. The one occupant, Charlie, sat at a table but he was not reading. He was looking at the fireplace, a gentle, thoughtful expression on his face. This was a Charlie Em had not seen before.

She walked across the room. He looked up. "Has your reporter friend gone?" She nodded. "Well, I have something to tell you." He stood up. "Something my father has stirred up. I got home yesterday and found that he wants to provide some kind of memorial to your brother Ashton and wants me to decide what."

"A memorial to Ashton! The judge!" Em exclaimed in surprise. "I wonder what made him decide that."

"He wouldn't tell me. Said I'd find out soon. I've just been sitting here, Em, looking at that big space above the fireplace. To me it is just crying out for a beautiful picture to hang there. Do you remember that painting that was on exhibit here in December, the big one called 'Autumn in Brown County'?"

"Why, yes, I do," Em answered. "It was my favorite."

"Well, I saw it again at another exhibit in Indianapolis. Now what would you think of Father getting that to hang here in the library as a memorial to Ashton?"

"Oh, Charlie, that would be—! But that painting is so very expensive." Em looked at the space above the fireplace.

"Father wants to do it. I told him about the picture and I came over today to see if this spot would be as right for it as I remembered."

"I told Ashton about that painting," Em said thoughtfully. "Autumn was his favorite time of year. His birthday was in October."

"Yes, I remember." Charlie glanced down at her. "And so is yours." He looked directly into her eyes.

Em's heart gave a sudden pound. Was he remembering their walk in the rain?

"Well, now that the painting has your approval, could you walk over to Miss Buchanan's with me to find out what she thinks of the idea?"

"I suppose I can. I'll telephone home before we leave. But what about Papa and Mama? They should have a say-so on this."

"Father and I called on them early this afternoon. They are agreeable. Father wants this settled today so he can write to the art gallery in the morning."

Em glanced at her watch. "It's nearly time to leave. I'll call home."

"I'll see you at the front door." Charlie picked up his hat and coat.

Before leaving, Em took a last look at the fireplace, imagining the autumn scene above. What a nice thing for the judge to do. What was it Papa had called him? An old windbag? Papa was going to have to eat those words.

The walk with Charlie to Miss Buchanan's was delightful. Spring was everywhere: forsythia bushes yellow as sunlight, lilac blooms fragrant and beautiful, apple trees budding pink, and the smell of damp earth and its growing greenery filling the air.

Miss Buchanan welcomed them and when Charlie explained the reason for their visit, she beamed with pleasure.

"Well, well, what a great thing for the judge to do. Over the fireplace you say." She pursed her lips and nodded. "Exactly the place. I tell you what, we'll have a special dedication ceremony right there in the reading room, maybe on a Sunday afternoon. And we'll get that reporter friend of yours, Emmy, to write it up for the *News.* What is his name?"

"Jim Addison."

"Oh, yes, Mr. Addison. We should get some fine publicity for the library. Charlie, how long will you be home?"

"A week. I leave next Sunday."

"Well, it's *good* to see you, Charlie. Your idea for the picture is wonderful. That particular painting is lovely! Em, did you have a chance to show him the new charging desk in the children's room?"

"No, I didn't, Miss Buchanan."

"You must come in next week and have a good look around. Did Em tell you we have another staff member?"

"No."

Em spoke up hurriedly. "Molly Flannery is on the staff now. I believe you know her." She watched his face closely.

"Molly? Well, what do you know! I wouldn't have figured her for a librarian."

Now what did he mean by that? That Molly was too pretty? "Why not?" Em asked sharply.

"Oh, I don't know."

"Now, Charles," Miss Buchanan put in, "you must know that all librarians don't have to look like or be like me. I have three of the prettiest and smartest girls in Harper City on my staff. And Emeline Dudley here is a shining combination of the beauty and brains our library requires."

Em laughed and blushed at the praise. Bless dear Jenny Buchanan! "Now, Miss Buchanan, don't turn my head with words like that. I might feel too uppity to read shelves in the morning."

"I'm not worried. Doc Dudley's daughter keeps her feet on the ground. Charlie, you should see the way Em handles

the work in the children's room. And the children are growing so fond of her."

Charlie gave Em a long look and said, "I shouldn't
wonder." He smiled. "I expect if I didn't have to go back
to school, I'd start reading the Henty books again."

On Tuesday, about half-past four, with the evening
News in her hand, Miss Buchanan stepped into the
children's room. Em was seated at the charging desk,
putting book cards into the pockets of the books just returned.

"Wanted you to see this before I put it in the reading
room." The librarian spread the paper on the desk and
opened it to the second page.

Em looked. "Why for goodness sake! A picture of Ashton
and one of Charlie."

"Yes. Your Mr. Addison has done a fine piece on the
war. A lot of it he has written from your father's point of
view, and from the judge's, too."

"I wonder how he got Ashton's picture."

"From your father, I expect. He quotes from an interview
he had with Maylen, and also he talked with the judge."
Miss Buchanan refolded the paper. "I must put this in the
reading room before old Mr. Earl starts complaining. He's
the one who goes into the reading room at four o'clock
and stares accusingly at the charging desk until we put
the paper in there."

"I know. He comes on Sunday too."

Miss Buchanan nodded. "This library is the only pleasure
he has. His family is gone and he lives in one room over
Crawley's grocery store. I mustn't keep him waiting."

Em watched the librarian leave. She would read that as
soon as she got home. She wondered why the reporter
hadn't used the picture of Charlie in his uniform.

After supper that evening the doctor read Jim Addison's article aloud to the whole family.

The story was headlined, "Remember the *Maine* and Ashton Dudley." It began:

Among some recently published letters written by notables during the war is one written last year by the United States Ambassador to England, John Hay, to Colonel Theodore Roosevelt, at present the Governor of New York. The Ambassador wrote, "It has been a splendid little war; begun with the highest motives, carried on with magnificent intelligence and spirit, favored by that fortune which loves the brave."

The war may have been splendid for many people but not for the family of Ashton Dudley, who died last December as a result of yellow fever contracted in Cuba. Nor was it splendid to those who sweltered in that island's tropical heat and faced the Spanish bullets, many of them dying in agony on dirty, bloody battlefields.

One year ago today Congress declared war on Cuba.

Jim Addison went on to give a short résumé of the war, then returned to Ashton. At one point Em interrupted her father to ask, "Papa, how did he know all that about Ashton?"

The doctor looked at her over his spectacles. "I told him. The judge brought him to my office one afternoon and the three of us talked. I gave him this picture, too."

The article quoted the judge's story of how Ashton had rescued his son Charles from the battlefield and how the young medic's persistence had saved his son's arm.

When Dr. Dudley finished, no one spoke for a long while, thoughts of Ashton filling their minds. Mama broke the silence. "Maylen, I think Judge Hargrove is a very fine man."

Her husband folded the paper. "He is indeed, Nellie. And I take back all the things I've said about him."

"And, Papa," Em said, "it was Charlie who thought of that painting for the library in memory of Ashton."

The doctor smiled gently. "Yes, daughter. And I take back what I've said about him too. From what the judge told me, Charlie has settled down and is determined to make something of the life Ashton saved." He put the newspaper on the table and looked down at Vic, seated on the floor, his dog in his arms. "Son, how about going down for office hours with me. I have some work laid out for you."

Mama and Em exchanged glances as the two Dudley "men" left the room. At last the real Papa had returned.

The next day Em went to the newspaper office and bought another copy of last night's paper. That evening, in her room, she clipped the two pictures and article and put them in the Lowney's Bonbon box along with the three letters from Charlie and the picture of him in his Rough Rider uniform.

Chapter 18

Twentieth Century Ahead!

On Sunday afternoon, May 28, a group gathered in the reading room at the library. A large cloth covered the space above the fireplace.

The tables pushed back, rows of folding chairs had been set up. Em sat with her family in the front row. Mrs. Hargrove, the judge, Charlie, and Miss Buchanan sat behind them. The mayor, the City Council, and the Library Board were present, as well as the other staff members and their families.

Em listened to the speeches: one by Mr. Roxberry, who had known Ashton from his early Sunday School days, one by the mayor, one by Mr. Long of the Library Board, and a surprisingly short, sincere, simple one by the judge.

At a sign from the judge, Vic rose from beside the doctor and pulled at the cord hanging by the fireplace. The covering aside, "Autumn in Brown County" was revealed in all of its colorful beauty.

After a few minutes of silence, the minister said a prayer, then a benediction. The people rose, some leaving at once, others coming closer to the picture.

Em and Mama stepped nearer to read the bronze plaque the judge had had placed under the picture.

GIVEN IN MEMORY OF ASHTON DUDLEY
HIS SPIRIT LIVES ON IN ALL WHO KNEW HIM

Mama nodded. "So true, so true. Everyone loved Ashton." Charlie approached. "A very nice ceremony, Charles.
What will you be doing this summer?"

"In two weeks I go back to Bloomington for summer
school. I've lost a lot of time, and have so much to make
up, Mrs. Dudley." He glanced at Em. She smiled.

Molly Flannery had been in the audience, but she had
left with her family. Charlie hadn't even looked at Molly.
At home there were four more letters in the bonbon box.
Em had relaxed as far as Molly was concerned. Working
with her everyday, she and Molly had become even better
friends. Molly seemed as intent on becoming a good librarian
as she, herself, was, Em decided.

On Sunday, the fourth of June, Charlie took Em for a
ride in the Hargrove buggy. They drove out to the City
Park, tied the horse and walked around, watching families
at picnic gatherings and children running and playing on
the grounds.

Before returning to the buggy, the two stopped at the
roaring artesian well and drank from tin cups that hung
on long chains. Getting a good, cold, Park drink was something one always did before leaving.

Charlie helped Em into the buggy. Seated on the other
side of her, he gave her a long look. Em returned it without faltering.

"Emmy, you get prettier every day." He unwound the
reins from the whip socket, pulled on them to back away
from the hitching rail. "Sometimes I wonder if I'm real
smart to go off and leave you this summer. I saw that

reporter fellow, Jim what's-his-name, at the library affair last Sunday. Does he come in often?"

"Jim Addison? He comes about once a week to see if we have any news items for him. The library is part of his beat." Em smiled as she pulled on a glove. "One of the biggest library news items, we can't tell him yet. Jessie is quitting at the end of July to marry Alex Thompson!"

"Well, what do you know! Good old Alex!"

"Yes, he has done very well with his bicycle shop. He is adding a second floor to the shop and they'll live up there."

Charlie nodded. "Very nice. Em, you know I often question all this going-to-school business. It takes so long. Now Alex and Jessie are able to get married before they get to be old folks. Why, it will be years before I can settle down. I'll be an old man."

Em laughed. "Let's see, you were just nineteen, so you'll be twenty-two or -three before you finish up—really ancient. But seriously, Charlie, you must keep on at the University. Think of Ashton and of the years he put in studying medicine."

Charlie sighed. "I know. With you and my parents urging me, I don't suppose I dare quit."

"I've got some plans of my own," Emmy said, folding her gloved hands in her lap. "I'm saving my money to go to library school in Chicago next summer. With Jessie leaving, I can't go this summer, but Miss Buchanan is sure that I may next year."

"Say, that's good!" Charlie exclaimed. "How long a course is it?"

"Six weeks. It's the same one Miss Buchanan attended several years ago. She says it will mean more to me because I will have had practical experience in a library." Em reached up and pushed the long hatpin farther into the crown of her straw sailor. "This summer I want to make some special plans for the children's room for the fall when school starts again."

"What kind of plans?"

"Well, yesterday morning the Garden Club's executive committee met in one of the small meeting rooms. I went up to unlock it for them. Afterward I noticed the door to the auditorium was open so I stepped in. Mr. Stewart was washing windows. I stood there and looked at the empty seats and the stage. And all at once I could see those front seats filled with children and myself telling them stories. You remember I did that last November when the children moved the books. The first few times I wasn't very sure of myself, but after a while I grew to enjoy it and the more I enjoyed the telling the more interested the children became." Em stopped and gave a contented sigh. "Charlie, there is nothing as satisfying as telling a tale when you feel that the children are living in that tale as completely as you are!"

Charlie pulled on the reins and slowed the horse to a walk. "Em, I bet you're a great storyteller."

"I'm not really, but I intend to be. Yesterday I talked to Miss Buchanan about telling stories every so often in our library hall. She said come fall I could try it out and see how it works. And you know what, Charlie?" Em turned to him, her face bright with enthusiasm. "That stage would be wonderful for little plays for special holidays like Christmas and Halloween. I didn't mention *that* to Miss Buchanan. I'll have to succeed with story hours first."

"Emmy Lou Dudley, I do believe you like your work! Maybe it's a good thing I'm going back to school. If I were here I'd just have to play second fiddle to Harper City's children."

Em leaned back and looked at the dusty road stretching ahead of the horse. "I'll always have time for you, Charlie," she said softly.

Em's summer was a full one. Miss Buchanan decided that every book in the library must be inspected for needed mending, those with loose backs to be put aside for rebinding; at eighteen cents a book, she said, it was money well spent. The staff also took inventory to determine what books had disappeared.

"I have been asked to speak at the Indiana Library Association meeting in October on the subject of 'Open Shelves,'" she told her staff. "Not many libraries permit patrons to walk freely in the stacks to select their own books. We have had open shelves for four years, now, and I certainly would not want to go back to closed shelves. This inventory will show us just how many books we have lost in that time."

Inventory showed that, in four years, only seven books had been lost and three of those had been paid for. Miss Buchanan said the loss of four books in four years was a small price to pay for open shelves.

During August the library was closed on Sundays. Jessie and Alex were married on Sunday, August 6. As Em watched Jessie and Alex standing before the minister, she thought how Alex had changed. Engagement to Jessie had made him a stronger man; he held his broad shoulders erect with an air of confidence. Jessie had done this for him. Could she, herself, help Charlie in any way? she wondered.

The bonbon box was full of letters from Bloomington. She had answered them all. Charlie had never spoken of love, but he had poured out his thoughts to her in the letters, and she had put a lot of herself on paper in response. Perhaps she and Charlie learned more about one another through letters than they would have if they actually had been together. Ideas written were more likely to be serious than one's conversation face to face.

The first of September, Mrs. Enderis joined the library staff. She was a widow whose children had married and left town. Molly and Em found her a delightful person, witty, with a keen sense of humor and a store of funny family anecdotes to fit every occasion, and, she seemed to know every one in town.

Now, Em found herself "second in command." When Miss Buchanan went to Indianapolis in October, she put Miss Dudley in charge. Before leaving, Miss Buchanan taught her the combination of the safe, where the "fine" money from overdue books was kept along with certain important library papers. Em felt very set up the day the president of the Library Board asked her to open the safe for him so that he might look at certain insurance papers.

The last Saturday in October, Em held her first story hour for children in the library hall. Miss Buchanan had sent letters to all the schools, inviting the children, and Jim Addison had written a piece that appeared in Friday night's *News*. FIRST LIBRARY STORY HOUR TO BE CONDUCTED BY MISS EMELINE DUDLEY, the lines above the article stated. As Em read it aloud to her family she felt little shivers of fear creep up and down her backbone. She had prepared her program carefully, but what if—?

"May I come to hear you, Sis?" Vic asked.

"If you want to. You may be the only one there."

"Now, now, Emmy, you'll have a good audience with all that publicity." Mama reassured her. "You and Ashton were always telling stories to one another. You'll do fine. Remember what success you had almost a year ago when the children moved the books."

"Yes, but Miss Buchanan and the teacher were always present to take care of any discipline problems."

"Well, just think of how many children you know now and who know you. Just be your friendly self, relax and enjoy your story and the children will too."

Children began arriving at half-past one. Miss Buchanan sent Molly into the children's room to take over at the charging desk so that Em could go upstairs to supervise the children in the hall. She stood at the open door and listened to the shuffle of small feet on the marble steps and watched them file past her to the front rows. As the number grew and three rows were filled, her throat became dry with panic.

At the moment she could not think of one word of the three stories she had prepared! What would she do? And how could this be? For weeks and weeks she had worked on these particular stories, going out to the barn at home to rehearse them aloud.

"What time is it, Miss Dudley?" a small boy asked.

Em looked at her watch. "It is sixteen minutes to three, Tony."

"What time did you say the show would begin?"

"At three o'clock."

Oh, merciful heaven, a show! What were these children expecting? What would they do when the "show" turned out to be just one nineteen-year-old librarian, whose brown hair was fluffed up in a pompadour in front and coiled on top in a soft knot, who was dressed in a black skirt and a white, high-collared, eyelet embroidery shirtwaist, and who was armed with only the words of three stories with which to entertain them? And right now those words seemed to have lost themselves in the panic that had taken hold of her.

But, on second thought, the words of those stories were good ones, written by three capable authors, Hans Christian Andersen, Mary Wilkins Freeman, and Frank Stockton. Armed with the works of these, why was she afraid?

And yesterday was Ashton's birthday, surely a good omen just before this job she had undertaken. "You are the library," he had said. Then it was up to her to make this *story hour* the library too. It should be a way of making the library so attractive to these children that they would become lifelong friends and users of Mr. Carnegie's gift.

At three o'clock she closed the door and walked to the front of the hall. The children stopped conversation and watched her expectantly. Em hesitated. Should she stand in front of the stage as she had before, or up on it? There must be over two hundred children here, not like the small groups she had had before. Her storytelling would have to be different to reach them all. She mounted the steps and went to the center of the stage.

Clasping her hands just below her belt, she said, "Boys and girls, I am going to tell you a story by Hans Christian Andersen called 'The Tinder Box.' This story has three of the most amazing dogs in it that you will ever, ever hear about, even if you live to be a hundred and thirty-seven!"

The children laughed and Em launched into her story, describing the pictures that appeared in her mind, relating the conversation as the characters seemingly spoke to her inner ear. Wherever those words had been hiding, the sight of the eager eyes before her brought them forth in their proper, narrative order. By the time she got to the dogs whose eyes were as big as saucers, as big as millstones, and as big as the Round Tower, she was completely confident. The tale was as real to her as to the children.

At the end of the story she said, "Now, if anyone wants to leave, he may do so before I start the next story."

No one left and Em began "Ting-a-Ling's Visit to Turilira." She had worked very hard on this story, memorizing the name of the strange creature that Frank Stockton called the Kyrofatalapynx, until the word slipped off her tongue as easily as a simple one. How the children laughed when the fairy Ting-a-Ling, speaking to the giant Turilira, could not pronounce it and called it the Kyro-what-you-may-call-it.

Just before the end, Miss Buchanan tiptoed in and sat in a back seat. During the applause that followed the story, Em glanced her way and saw her nodding approval.

Now it seemed to Em that the children and she were one. It was the same sensation she used to have when she and Ashton were off on a game of let's pretend and both were living in the exciting, beautiful world created by their imaginations.

She didn't even stop to ask if anyone wanted to leave, but launched into "The Pumpkin Giant" with confidence and gusto.

Coming off the stage with the children clamoring for more, she vowed that some day she would have a head *full* of tales so she could go on and on. But, on second thought, it might be better to stop while they still wanted more. That way they would come again whenever she advertised story hour.

Miss Buchanan was waiting for her. Em, her face flushed with success, smiled shyly. "Was it all right, Miss Buchanan? May I do it again?"

The librarian squeezed her arm. "Emmy Lou, you are a *born* storyteller. You have the voice, the sparkle, a sense of the dramatic and the knack of letting others feel and see what your imagination is creating. I took a course in storytelling at library school, but no one can be taught what *you* were born with. Of course you may do it again. Now you better hurry down to the children's room and help Molly. She will be swamped. All this crowd should boost juvenile circulation today."

As Em went down the stairs she could almost hear Ashton saying, "Good girl, Emmy! You *were* the library."

It was during the Christmas story hour on December 23 that the entrance of a young man into the back of the auditorium nearly threw the storyteller into utter confusion. Hat and overcoat in hand he sat down and smiled broadly at her.

With difficulty she picked up the thread of her story, and soon was able to continue in her usual style. *Have* to do well, she thought, Charlie is here! And she did!

Walking downstairs beside him, children in front of them, children behind them, Em, still exhilarated by the storytelling, chattered animatedly to Charlie. "I was so surprised to see you I nearly forgot my story. When did you come home?"

"An hour ago. You know, Em Dudley, you are some storyteller. Almost like an actress, I'd say. What a spell you cast on the young ones. Where did you learn to do that?"

"A lot of it is just plain hard work. I have been working on stories since last June. Storytellers can't be too well prepared, to my way of thinking. Miss Buchanan says they are born, and by that I suppose she means they come by the gift of gab naturally. But honestly, Charlie, I'm surprised by the whole thing. I didn't know I could do it. It seems that when I get up there I just turn something on and out comes the story. It's a strange feeling; it's as though I am a medium through which the author sends out his creation. Kind of crazy, isn't it?"

They stopped on the lower landing.

"No. I think you explain it very well. I'm awfully proud of you, Em. May I take you for a sleigh ride tomorrow afternoon? There's just the right amount of snow."

Em nodded. "What time?"

"About three."

Charlie left and Em went into the crowded children's room, where a Christmas tree sparkled by the fireplace. She smiled at Molly, seated at the charging desk, then asked a boy:

"David, have you found a good book yet?"

There was a lilt to her voice; the tone sparkled as brightly as the tinsel on the tree. What a beautiful world! She had been blessed with a knack for telling tales and Charlie, home just an hour, had headed right for the library to hear her!

Em walked on air all the following week. There had been the sleigh ride on Sunday, Christmas on Monday, and Charlie walking her home from the library every day. On Christmas he had brought her a five-pound box of candy, Huyler's Bonbons this time. The box was even prettier than the first one, the one now so full of letters. She wondered how long it would take to fill the Huyler's box.

December 31, New Year's Eve, was on Sunday.

"Em, how about going to my church with me on New Year's Eve?" Charlie had asked. "I've got to leave first thing on Monday morning. Tad Wilson is meeting me in Indianapolis and we're going on to Bloomington together."

"All right," she had agreed. "Is Tad preparing you for exams?"

"That's right. He needs the money and I need the tutoring. I expect to do well this time, Emmy."

The New Year's Eve service in Charlie's church was over at half-past nine. Em had been impressed by the message.

"You are privileged," the minister had said. "You are on the threshold of the new century. The twentieth century lies ahead! Enter it prayerfully, praying that we use it well for the betterment of mankind. May we never get so involved with luxurious living the new century's inventions may bring that we forget that only the spirit of love for one another can give true satisfaction and meaning to our lives."

"You have a fine minister, Charlie," Em said on the way home.

"Yes, isn't he!"

"Charlie, you know it's kind of scary, being right here in the middle. We can look back at the eighteen-hundreds and point out the big happenings, like the wars we have had, the inventions that have come into use, such as the telephone, the telegraph, the gramophone, electricity, and the spread of the railroads across the land, and then there's the automobile. But Papa says *that* will never amount to anything. He says nothing will ever replace the horse for dependable transportation."

"I disagree. In time I expect your father may be making his house calls in an auto. The Haynes-Apperson Automobile Company in Kokomo did not go into business just for their health. I hear their cars are selling."

"Well, anyway, we know all about the nineteenth century; but up ahead, there is the twentieth, and we have only the haziest notion of what it will bring." Em paused and looked at the man beside her. Not able to see his face in the dark, she could see his features in her mind; clear as day, they were. What did the twentieth century hold for Charlie and her?

"I'm taking a course in English Literature, as you know," Charlie said. "We have to memorize a lot of poetry. Not knowing about the new century reminds me of a few lines by Bobbie Burns in 'To a Mouse.' He says:

> Still thou art blest, compared wi' me!
> The present only toucheth thee:
> But, och! I backward cast my e'e
>   On prospects drear!
> An' forward, tho I canna see,
>   I guess an' fear!"

"Well, I'm glad I'm not as morbid as Bobbie Burns," Em returned. "The nineteenth century was good to me in everything except that it took Ashton from us. And I'm not afraid of anything the twentieth has to offer. So there, that for your Bobbie Burns and his mouse!" Em tossed her head and laughed.

"I'm not afraid either, Emmy." He took her gloved hand from her muff and pulled it through the crook of his elbow. "I wish I could tell you, Em, dear, of all the plans I have for you and me. But I don't have the right, yet. It will be so long before I'm finished school and can tell the way I feel toward you. Will you wait until I can?"

"I'll wait, Charlie."

They stood for a moment on the front porch. He lifted Em's face and kissed her. "I'll think of you tonight when the bells ring in the new century, our century. Will you think of me, Emmy?"

"I'll think of you, Charlie."

She watched him go down the walk and stood there

even after he disappeared. The street lamp and the snow threw a glow over the front yard.

There stood stalwart old Blitzen, the snow on his back like a blanket. Em's heart was beating faster than usual. He had kissed her. Now she was sure that for her the twentieth century was Charlie!

"Oh, Ashton, I wish you knew," she said softly. "Wherever you are, I wish you knew how happy I am."

Good girl, Emmy Lou, good girl!

About the Author

Elisabeth Hamilton Friermood has the happy faculty of writing books that both her readers and reviewers greet with enthusiasm. Most of her books have period settings, and many have the Midwest as a background. Her characterizations, plots, and period details "read as immediately and vividly as last week's news magazine." (*Christian Science Monitor*)

Mrs. Friermood, a native of Marion, Indiana, studied at Northwestern University and the University of Wisconsin, and was children's librarian in Marion and Dayton, Ohio, before moving to New York in 1944. The Friermoods have a married daughter, Libby.

BOOKS BY ELISABETH HAMILTON FRIERMOOD

Ballad of Calamity Creek

Candle in the Sun

Doc Dudley's Daughter

Geneva Summer

Head High, Ellen Brody

Hoosier Heritage

Jo Allen's Predicament

The Luck of Daphne Tolliver

Promises in the Attic

"That Jones Girl"

The Wabash Knows the Secret

Whispering Willows

The Wild Donahues

52650

J
Fri
~~WITHDRAWN~~

Friermood, Elisabeth H.

Doc Dudley's daughter.